Haunted Journey

RUTH RIDDELL

Haunted Journey

Atheneum   1988   New York

Atheneum
Macmillan Publishing Company
866 Third Avenue, New York, NY 10022
Collier Macmillan Canada, Inc.
First Edition   Designed by Marjorie Zaum
Printed in USA
10   9   8   7   6   5   4   3   2   1

Library of Congress Cataloging-in-Publication Data
Riddell, Ruth.
Haunted journey/by Ruth Riddell.—1st ed.   p.   cm.
Summary: To pay off the taxes on his late father's land, Obie
travels to the haunted River Country in hopes of finding pearls
in the mussel beds.   ISBN 0-689-31429-9
[1. Country life—Fiction. 2. Pearls—Fiction.] I. Title.
PZ7.R4166Hau 1988   [Fic]—dc19   88-938   CIP   AC

For my mother, Beulah Nugent, who knew the Wilks family, about life up the holler. And for Kathleen Phillips, a good friend and gentle critic.

"When a trout rising to a fly gets hooked on a line and finds himself unable to swim about freely, he begins with a fight which results in struggles and splashes and sometimes an escape. Often, of course, the situation is too tough for him.

"In the same way the human being struggles with his environment and with the hooks that catch him. Sometimes he masters his difficulties; sometimes they are too much for him. His struggles are all that the world sees and it naturally misunderstands them. It is hard for a free fish to understand what is happening to a hooked one."

Karl A. Menninger

Haunted Journey

CHAPTER

1

✳ ✳ ✳

AN EMPTY BELLY, BLISTERED FEET AND A HEAD FULL OF doubts were immediately forgotten when a break in the trees opened a corridor to the upper reach of a rocky knob. Each boy looked at the other: Was this the place they had traveled so far to find? They shouted for Chaser to follow and ran the remaining distance.

"Lawd-a-mighty!" Obie sucked in his breath and grabbed his dog by the neck to keep her from slipping over the edge.

Several hundred feet below where he stood rested a short, skinny valley, colored as brilliantly as the late evening sunset that set the western sky ablaze. Hemlocks grew from crevices in the steep-sided ridge and stood dark green among yellow poplars. High on the distant hill, spruce and fir trees reached into the darkening October sky.

Obie's gaze moved slowly down the hillside to the

river below. It flowed through a dense forest and between dead and disfigured trees, a roosting place for buzzards who perched on the old skeletons to watch. Was this a valley that once belonged to Cherokees, a place De Soto explored? Was this the River Country his great-granddaddy Wilks told so many stories about? Was this how it looked back in 1800 when Micager Wilks kept company with the likes of Dan'l Boone?

Obie looked again at the yellow and frayed paper he pulled from his pocket. He studied the fading lines of the old map, then the stretch of land that lay below. He wanted to say something reassuring to the boy who stood beside him. They had traveled so far, followed the map so carefully. It had been one hundred and thirty years since Micager drew the map. Things changed in that length of time. But the map and its directions had brought them to this place. Should he trust that? If they were to continue in search of a place that matched the lines on the map, they would move deeper into a wilderness inhabited by Cherokee spirits, Indian burial grounds and legendary ghosts. To this day his uncle Hassel swore that the people of the Nun Yuna Wi kept careful watch over the mussel beds where the Sallapoosa and Yuda rivers joined. He swore that the valley remained a wilderness because those who foolishly trespassed its bounds met with a horrible fate. His uncle Hassel was a churchgoing man, read from the Bible every night. Should he heed his uncle's warnings or was it all superstition, story talk?

Obie let the air from his lungs slowly in hopes of ridding his thoughts of the foreboding welling within him. He refused to betray the reason that had brought him so far from home or the boy who asked to share his adventure. He could not allow all the misgivings, now yelling for attention, to persuade him to turn back. Tomorrow they would look for the place where the two rivers joined.

Obie refolded the map. His hand, as he withdrew it from the deep pocket, brushed the silky hair along Chaser's scarred, bony frame. This half Blue Tick, half Georgia Redbone was the best tracking, best cat and bear dog in the county. She would find her way back to Wilks Hollow; he would see his sisters and brothers again, his mamma, too. And he would prove wrong what she had said, *"You got about as much chance of finding a pearl as you got of finding pie in the sky."*

Obie leaned out over the ledge to study the sand- and rock-strewn arm that rested alongside the river. Behind them and cut into the limestone ledge lay a line of shallow caves that offered a safe place for sleeping. But Obie wanted to try his hand at pearling and looked for a way down. "There's a likely spot right below," he said to Bas. "We can spend the night there."

"Then this here ain't the place we come to find?"

"It's the Sallapoosa all right, but we need to be finding where it joins the Yuda."

Obie slapped his leg and Chaser followed. "Long as the light holds out I aim to be looking for our first pearl."

"Sounds good to me, then we won't have to go no farther than right here. Ain't that right?"

"Nope, we come to find the mussel beds my great-gran'daddy told about and this here ain't the place."

"Dang it, Obie! How come you're so cussed stubborn?" Not meaning to have spoken so loudly, Bas looked out from beneath the brim of his hat and glanced over his shoulder. "If there's a-body close by," he whispered, "he shore knowd he ain't by hisself."

They picked their way across the slant-sided ridge wall carefully. Only the sound of an occasional rock that slipped from beneath their bare feet and bounced against the ledge echoed through the silence. They dropped the last ten feet onto the sand- and rock-strewn arm that reached into the river.

A darkening chill prompted Obie to open his tow sack and dump the contents. His shoes fell out first. His coat smelled of lard fat and pone but the scents of home succumbed to the whirlpool of river odors and decay. He buttoned the coat to his neck, pulled the scratchy collar around his ears.

Chaser sniffed the ground as she ran the length of the sandy shelf, sniffed the edge of grayback boulders that lay here and there on the sand like long-forgotten tombstones. Her nose twitched as she returned to Obie's side. He felt her body quiver. She growled a low sound that told him she found it impossible to see into the darkness, too, that the scent she detected was an unfamiliar one, that there was something out there in the dark, hiding from her.

"You can be building us a fire," Obie said and pointed back to where the sand touched the ledge and turned reddish brown.

"You reckon someone lives hereabouts?"

"Not likely. This is wilderness."

"What about the Cherokees that scattered over these here hills?"

"That was eighty or ninety years ago. Reckon they're all dead by now."

4

"You knowd that for certain?"

"No, but—"

"Then it's possible that there's a Cherokee or two in these here hills."

"Anything's possible, but—"

"That's all I were asking." Bas dropped his tow sack and propped his rifle alongside.

"Come on, girl." Obie slapped his leg for Chaser to follow but she ran ahead to the river. It flowed deep and dark. On the other side trees crowded close to the edge and made a high, solid wall. Luckily there had been frosty nights, a cold spell and rain earlier in the month, killing off the army of mosquitoes that lived in the lush bottom.

Obie knelt down. He watched a leaf float past. The current and the amount of mud that swirled in little circles surprised him. Stories that he remembered from all of his near fifteen years convinced him that he would find pigtoe mussels in River Country and not the rough, irregular-shaped ripplebacks that favored the deep, slow-running, murky waters. He sat back on his heels, troubled over the many other things so many years of storytelling may have changed.

Obie picked up a small chunk of milky white quartz from the sand. He rolled it between his thumb and forefinger but his gaze focused upon the distant peaks and the black, irregular ribbons that separated one ridge from another. Ninety years seemed like a long time ago. Though members of his family had been living up Wilks Hollow for over one hundred years, the possibility of Cherokees still living here in the surrounding hills was remote. Not even Indians could survive in such a wilderness. He skipped the small chunk of rock across the water.

He turned from the river and began gathering wood. He looked for pieces less exposed to the river's dampness but stopped short of entering the woods. "If you build a fire and cook us up some supper"—Obie dropped the firewood beside Bas—"I'll get to finding us a pearl."

"Going in that there river ain't good sense," Bas said. "It's getting on to dark and it's cold as a witch's kiss."

While Bas set out to gather more wood, Obie rummaged through the contents of his tow sack—a rattle of pots and kettles, rope, quilt and clothes, shoes, knife and hatchet. He stretched the long coil of rope straight across the sand, then took a three foot length, found the center and tied it there to the longer piece. Next, he took from the clutter of odds and ends a small packet and laid back the folds of newspaper. Rather than centering his attention upon the short threads of wire inside the packet, Obie stared at the face looking up at him. "Mr. President Hoover," he said, "a man who don't keep to his promises is a no-account liar. 'Cause of you us Wilkses is in a lick of trouble."

"Who you talking to?" Bas added more wood to the pile.

"Him!" Obie jabbed his finger at the picture of Herbert Hoover. "He give his word to help out. Said that a man could go to the R.F.C. for work. Ain't so. I tried."

Obie crunched the newspaper into a wad. "Use it to light the fire," he said and began to push one thin wire after another through the three-foot section of rope.

"Whatcha call that contraption anyways?"

"Grappling line. River's too deep for wading and I can't see for the mud. I'll keep throwing this out and dragging it back until I hook some ripplebacks."

"How you figure to hook mussels with them wires?" Bas stuffed the newspaper beneath a pile of twigs and dry leaves.

"It's not the wire that catches the mussels; it's the mussels that catch the wires. You know how they stand upright on the blade of their shell so their hinge is turned up, don't you?"

"I've seen them that a-way."

"They'll suck up whatever happens along. It'll be a natural thing for them to catch hold of the wire, thinking it's something to eat." Obie looped the long coil around his arm. "Take hold, will you, Bas."

They started toward the water. Obie stopped. "Go back, Chaser. Don't you be running off neither."

At the river's edge Bas let his end of the rope drop and stepped aside as Obie swung the line toward the water. It shot across the murky surface, hit; the remainder uncoiled. He waited for it to sink out of sight but it lay on top and the current carried it downstream. Obie drew the line back; the grappling wires hung empty. After throwing it out another time, he moved upstream to the farthest reach of sand and prayed that he would find at least one mussel for a sign.

Of all the thinking and planning Obie had done before leaving home it had never occurred to him that the Sallapoosa might be different from the clear and fast moving streams near Wilks Hollow. The only way he would be able to use the grappling line in this river was to weight it with something that would take the wires to the bottom. Wood floated; a rock . . . ?

How would he attach a rock to the line? "Dang rain," he muttered. October was too early for the likes of

7

the storm that had made its way north the previous week and turned the river muddy. Made the sucking pots impossible to see, too.

Smoke from Bas's fire curled into the darkening sky. Obie took the familiar scent deep into his lungs. Rather than go back, he threw the long coil of rope another time. He watched it hit, watched it settle, watched the current carry it downstream. After a minute he pulled it back.

"Catch any of them mussels yet?" Bas yelled. "Them's good vittles."

Obie shook his head. The only thing he had to show for his efforts was a head full of doubts.

"Got coffee boiling and hoecakes roasting. Give it up, Obie. Ain't gonna do no good being out there when it's near dark as a dead man's eyes."

Obie fought against such reasoning but finally coiled the rope over his shoulder. Just as he turned he saw a shadow flit across the upper ridge, then disappear as suddenly as a falling star. Small, brownish, swift. Obie stood perfectly still, only his gaze crept toward the ledge. A cat, bear, wild boar? Obie licked his lips. Could it have been an Indian? A Nun Yuna Wi?

"Obie," Bas called, "what's keeping you?"

"Just looking," Obie called out, then whistled his way back to the fire. He set the rope aside. "I'm hungry as a bumblebee caught in a dry gourd. Think I could eat a barrel of them hoecakes."

Bas sat with his back to the ledge, his daddy's rifle resting across his knees. "Didn't find no mussels, huh?"

"I need to weight the line like I'd do to bottom fish." Obie turned his back on the fire. His shadow stretched across the sand before melting into the black wall that

8

only a mixture of sounds penetrated. "Chaser, come on over here." Obie dropped to his knees. "That coffee smells fine."

"It's hot," Bas replied, "but it doesn't taste so fine. River water were all that I could find."

"You saying there's no springs nearby?"

"Not that I could see from this here spot." Bas pulled the doeskin bag of rifle shells close to his side. "Molasses sweetens the coffee but it don't hide the muddy taste in them hoecakes."

Obie crawled around the fire and settled himself beside Bas. The heat seeped through the coat fibers and warmed his flesh. He pulled a hoecake from the coals, folded back the corn husks and blew on the steaming mixture of cornmeal, salt and boiled river water. He bit through the golden crust with some misgivings. Admittedly it tasted different from his mamma's but it was more satisfying than raw turnips.

Obie coaxed Chaser closer with the promise of a hoecake. She ate two more and Obie finished seven. "Tomorrow," he said, "you can find us a sweet spring and fresh meat."

"Mess of mussels would make tasty eating, too."

"I'll find them." Obie ran his hand across Chaser's head and listened to the sound of water rippling against the riverbank, crickets chirring and shrews on their nightly search. Other sounds he failed to identify made him scrunch his neck deeper inside his coat.

"Shore is dark," Bas said, and his hand moved along the butt of his rifle.

"Glad that your daddy let you bring along that gun. I can already taste roasted squirrel, maybe even some wild

9

turkey." Obie took another piece of wood from the pile and placed it over the flames. "Remember the turkey you shot behind the schoolhouse? Shot its head clean off."

"Got me a gray fox last spring. Dropped that varmint with my first shot." Bas rubbed the walnut stock affectionately. Without warning he jerked the rifle to his shoulder, squinted into the dark and aimed.

"What is it?" Obie's arm shot out; he grabbed Chaser by the ear. "What's out there?"

"Nothing," Bas answered and lowered the rifle. He laid it back across his knees. "Just wanted to show you how fast I was."

"Dang you! Near scared me spitless."

Bas grinned. He settled back, yet his forefinger rested alongside the trigger. "I never asked where you heared about that farmer in Traskville, the one that found the pearl in his posthole."

"Read about it in the newspaper. Mrs. Middleton gets a new one every week from Nashville."

"You believe such a farfetched story as that?"

"It was in the newspaper," Obie said. "It wouldn't have been there if it hadn't been true."

"Seems a mite blowed up to me."

"It only seems strange because you don't go to school and learn about things going on in the world."

"I went to school once. But that teacher took to deep talk and using big words, so I took to the woods. Told my daddy I weren't thoughted enough for schooling." Bas crossed one long leg over the other. "Did that newspaper tell the worth of that pearl?"

"Said in the neighborhood of one thousand dollars."

"Lawzzzie!" His grin stretched ear to ear. "I never

knowd there were something worth that much money. You reckon we can find us one of them kind?"

Obie nodded. "I showed you the one that my great-gran'daddy brought back from this place."

"What you showed me were a trifling, wee-bitty thing."

"That wee-bitty thing is worth fifty dollars if it's worth a dime."

"Who said?"

"Me. I know, like I know that we're going to find the mussel beds my great-gran'daddy saw when he was here. They'll be full of pigtoes, just like he said, too." Obie stirred the fire. "If my great-gran'daddy's story isn't true, you tell me why he went to all the trouble of making a map to lead him back to the exact spot that we're going to find?"

Obie reached into his pocket but Bas said, "No need to show me that thing again." And he turned toward the river when the ominous hooting of an unseen owl slithered through the shadows.

Goose bumps crawled up Obie's flesh as he searched the darkness before saying, "Did I tell you about the days when my daddy was a boy and folks were finding pearls in near every river and branch?"

"I heared them stories. Heared them more than once."

"They're not just stories; they're true," Obie said. "Nearly every stream had mussel beds but folks cleaned them out. Hasn't been nary a pearl found since those days."

"How come you think we'll find us a mess?"

"We'll find them because this is a secret place known

to nobody but us Wilkses." Obie cocked his head. "If you don't believe we're going to find pearls, how come you asked yourself along?"

Bas looked into the fire. "You knowd why."

Obie pressed his lips together, nodded. Yes, he knew why. Quickly smiling, he asked, "You ever heard about the men who came to Tennessee long before Dan'l Boone crossed over from Kentucky? Spanish men they were; one in particular was a soldier called De Soto. He explored near every river in the south."

Obie added another stick to the fire. He reached for a second, wanting a more brilliant blaze, but eyed the size of the pile with concern. Daylight remained hours off. They needed a fire to see them through the night. No telling the number or size of the predators prowling the darkness, and he withdrew an empty hand. "Do you know what a legend is?"

Bas pulled his hat low onto his forehead while Obie explained: "It's a story about real folks, real places, true happenings that took place a long while back. But the telling down through the years scrambles the facts like they were eggs."

Bas leaned back. His eyelids dropped, popped open. "If you're going to sleep," Obie said, "I'll not waste my breath telling you."

"I'm hearing. Dang smoke burns my eyes, that's all."

Obie studied him with careful consideration before continuing: "Four, maybe five hundred years back, De Soto came up this river from Caroliney, looking for gold. Instead of gold De Soto and his soldiers stumbled on a band of Cherokees. They treated the Indians real neighborly until they seen the lay of things." Obie poked a stick at the coals, trying to recall his daddy's exact words. "When De Soto got the upper hand, he made slaves of the Indians, stole their womenfolk, ransacked their villages looking for riches. One time, right here on the Sallapoosa—"

Bas's eyes popped open; he peered across the fire from beneath the brim of his hat, while Obie went on: "They met up with an old Indian queen in one of the villages. That woman come a-sashaying down to greet them, wearing a string of pearls strung five times around her fat neck and a-ways past her belly button."

"This here ain't a story from them books you're always reading, is it?"

"I'm telling you just what my daddy told me and his daddy told him." Obie paused. From the very bottom of his tow sack, he withdrew an old quilt and wrapped it around his shoulders before continuing: "When them Spaniards saw the pearls their eyeballs spun sixteen times inside their sockets and turned somersaults. One night, after real careful considering, they snuck up on the old queen while she was sleeping. Ripped them pearls right off of her fat neck. The whole lot of them black-hearted varmint lit off down river like beggar lice. That's when the chief called up to the spirits."

"Spirits?" Bas shook his head. "If you're fixing to tell that story your daddy used to tell, I ain't listening." He pulled down his hat. "Reckon what I want most is to sleep some."

Obie slid his arm around Chaser and tucked his fingers under her belly. He intended to keep the fire burning while Bas slept but the bright glow and warmth made his eyes heavy. Obie yawned. He pushed his butt close against the cold rock wall and made himself sit straight. Never in his life had he heard so many different night sounds, sounds that seemed to creep closer and closer. Obie's granddaddy once said, *"If a feller ever goes to River Country and plans on coming out alive, then he best learn to sleep with one eye open."*

Obie had never slept with just one eye shut but he did plan on returning to Wilks Hollow . . . alive.

CHAPTER
2
* * *

"... *WHAT I'M TELLING YOU, GRANDSON, IS PURE GOSPEL,* *told me by my daddy, your great-gran'daddy, Micager Wilks, who went to River Country, went there in the days of Dan'l Boone.*

"When them Spaniards stole the queen's pearls, the old Cherokee chief lifted his eyes to the spirits and cried out a bloodletting scream, painted hisself top to bottom, even used gunpowder to prick his chest with queer faces. Then he took to dancing and chanting through the night. Sun didn't show its face that next morning. No sirree, that day dawned dark as inside a Melungeon's heart. Thunder and lightning shook the earth for a hundred mile in every direction. Rained steady four day and five night; rivers flooded every holler around. The storm ripped hundred-year-old trees out by their roots, drowned all sort of four-legged critters, washed away more folk than anyone knowd for certain.

"Every Cherokee up and down the Sallapoosa and all its

branches were a-watching for them foreign buzzards. No way they was gonna escape back to Caroliney with all them pearls. But it weren't no living, breathing Cherokee that caught up with them. It were a Nun Yuna Wi, Grandson. And that ornery old mischief-maker waited until a full moon before he churned up the rivers. Made waves more fierce than the waves on the ocean, caused more commotion than a tornado. Caught them thieving rascals in their canoes and swept them out into the middle of the river. Downstream a-ways a cloud of black fog spread from one bank to the other. Then this big grizzly geyser, blood red it was, shot up in the air higher than any chestnut standing. When it fell back, it hit with such cussed orneriness that it made the Untigubi. The canoes and all them thieving vermin was pulled into the swirling current of the sucking pot. The water and them in it started going in a broad, fat circle. The more they spun around the faster they went. The closer they come to that sucking Untigubi the more they yelled, cried they did for their no-account hides. Then them boats butted heads with the heart of the sucking pot. It busted them to wee-bitty splinters, gobbled up them Spaniards faster than a turkey swallers grasshoppers. Sucked them clean down to the bottom of the river. Nobody ever knowd if it opened up so them devils could see the Immortals before they died. But it were about that time the earthquakes started. They caused every river here abouts to near crack in half. When the storm finally quieted and the water settled to where a feller could see, out come this pigtoe, come crashing out from a hole in the mountain. A pigtoe bigger than any jackass, milk cow or three sow hogs. That thing opened its jaws wider than the great lick is long, swallered up them foreigners and all they stole.

"Them Spaniards never got back to Caroliney. Not a single trace of them was ever found. Awhile after the ruckus, all the rivers calmed right quiet but that sucking pot's still hiding in the river and so's that cave down by the narrows. My daddy told me hisself that he seen the giant pigtoe, said it was bigger than Jacob's Knob.

"To protect the pigtoe beds from other pearl thieves, the Nun Yuna Wi gave peculiar powers to one among them called the stone man. That old one has got skin like lizzard hide, hard as any rock. Besides his body being twisted, he's got hair like sand myrtle and a face wrinkled as a horse apple. He carries what looks to be a twisted stick except it's made from pure marble. Just by aiming the thing, he's changed the course of rivers, set forests to burning, opened cracks in the earth; but the most terrible thing he does is turn men to stone.

"The year my daddy went to River Country with his friend Dan'l, he knowd about the stone man and the Nun Yuna Wi. But he weren't skeered. He owned good dogs and a new flintlock. When him and his friends come on the burying mound, they found more mussel shells than would fill Wilks Holler top-to-bottom. But they seen other sights, too. In the forest that surrounded the burying mound they seen the bones of grown men bleached white. Heard fellers a-screaming, seen big yeller eyes looking at them from the dark, smelled the stink of dead men. But your great-gran'daddy were a man of determination. Soon as he seen the mussel bed he tore off his breeches and jumped in. First mussel he cut into bore him a pearl. That's when the stone man swooped down out of the hills like a turkey buzzard.

"The old devil turned every one of the dogs to stone. Killed seven of your great-gran'daddy's closest friends with burning pine splinters shot from the end of that marble stick. Lucky for you, Obadiah Wilks, that Micager escaped the river and the sucking pot before it took him down.

"Being a thoughty man, Micager drew hisself a map of

the place, intending to go back. But when he got home he were a changed man. Took to churchgoing, Bible reading, even give up moonshine on the most festive of occasions. Sometimes he talked about going back. Took out his pearl, rolled it between his fingers, studied his map, but he never left Wilks Holler, contented he was to live an idlesome life till the day he died."

Obie opened his eyes. Instead of his granddaddy's voice, he heard river water gurgling and wind moaning through pines high on the ridge. It had been a dream, all of it no more real than story talk. A chill crept its way through Obie's shoulders and caused him to shiver. The map and pearl, safe inside his pocket, were real all right. Had it really been just a dream? Was the giant pigtoe, the cave, the Nun Yuna Wi just story talk?

Was it morning? He felt as if it should be. Instead of sleeping with one eye open, he had slept with both closed. Instead of sleeping upright, he had slept slumped over and his body ached. Instead of keeping a fire burning, he had let it die out. Only a faint warmth rose from the black coals. Afraid to move too quickly or rise, Obie turned slowly. The world around him remained black and he an outsider.

Bas . . . ? Obie listened for sounds of his companion's breathing. Other whispers made it impossible to be certain. He stretched his leg straight, moved it until he felt Bas's hand with his bare toes.

The hammering inside Obie's chest softened and he drew close to his dog. He pressed his face against her bony ribs. She smelled like dog, a good smell because it reminded him of home. "I love you," he whispered and wished that he was there asleep in the room he shared with his brothers, listening to Virg and Orvull snore, feeling Josh's heels kick his shinbone, smelling Caleb's pee. He wished that his daddy was alive. He wished that Virg was the oldest son.

Obie closed his eyes. He pressed the lids tight shut but not because he feared the dark and what might be lurking close by; cold tears stung his cheeks. He wished that instead of coming to River Country, he had gone north just like his uncle Tully had done years back, but being the oldest . . .

Obie tightened his arm around Chaser and drew her warmth closer. The hound's damp tongue passed over his fingers, a comforting sensation, and he kept his hand there so she would continue to lick. His daddy brought Chaser home for Obie's ninth birthday, found her alongside the road, hobbling on three feet. His mamma made a splint around her front leg and a bed for her beneath the stove. She tended to Chaser as carefully as she did her younguns. But the day the hound healed, she took a broom to her, called Chaser a pot-licker and shooed her from the house; would never hear of the dog coming back inside, not even on the coldest nights. But Chaser was better than a mongrel hound. She had breeding.

Obie's eyes drooped. He drifted off a second time. But when Chaser growled, Obie's eyes popped open. Daylight . . . Chaser squirmed free of his hold. She barked, bolted toward the river.

"Where is it?" Bas jerked the rifle to his shoulder as he raised to his knees.

"There," Obie said and pointed across the water.

A young doe browsed on the edge of the dense forest. Before Bas drew down and could pull the trigger, the deer darted back to safety. "Dang it!" Bas's lower lip shot out. "Another second and we'd be eating venison for breakfast."

"Not likely; no way we could get her across the river." Obie gathered sticks and dry leaves while Bas sank back on his haunches and watched.

"What time you figure it to be?"

Obie set the kindling over the coals and blew until a trickle of smoke curled upward. "Might be six. You hungry?"

"So hungry that my backbone's rubbing my belly button."

Obie poured last night's coffee into another pot, careful to leave the grounds and muddy sediment in the bottom. While it heated over the fire, he gathered more wood, expecting Bas to pitch in. Instead, Bas leaned back and crossed one big foot over the other.

"If you're so hungry," Obie said, "you can get off your rump and scare up a couple squirrels."

Bas's blond hair grew low on his neck and over his ears. His eyes, when they were open, showed blue and set deep inside a round face with stray hairs that might one day grow to be whiskers. Bas was older by several years, lived on Felker Mountain with his daddy, so he and Obie had never been more than speaking friends.

Now he stuck out his chin while his forehead turned into a deeply furrowed field. But he remained silent as Obie added rocks to an empty tow sack before heading upstream. He tied the sack of rocks near the end of the grappling line, certain that it would carry the wires to the bottom. Throwing it from the far end of the sand reach, Obie watched it splash down only a few feet out. For a moment he considered wading out and searching for mussels on the bottom, like he did along the branches at home. But the Sallapoosa was too high, the current too strong and faster than a flea could bite. He jumped back from the edge, aware that the soggy earth might give way beneath him.

Obie pushed his hands into his overall pockets. One held the pearl and his great-granddaddy's map. The other, his two quarters. He rubbed them together, knowing they were vital to his getting home. Obie stared at the mud swirling in the water, disagreeing now with his earlier decision to wait until October before traveling to River Country.

True, the heat and bugs were less; supposedly the rivers ran at their lowest; rains, the heavy ones, usually saved themselves for November. He had guessed wrong and it seemed to him that luck had turned its back on the Wilkses once again.

He squatted on his heels to watch the line. He knew Bas was sore but he refused to look back. He refused to consider the possibility of Bas lighting out for home and what being left alone would mean to him. If Bas should go, well . . .

Obie's vision glazed over as he fell to thinking: He was the first born, be fifteen the middle of November; he was responsible, just as his daddy had been made responsible when *his* daddy, Claiborne, got himself broken up in the flood of Nineteen 'n One. Obie tried to swallow; the lump in his throat felt melon size.

Just last spring he heard his daddy tell his uncle Hassel that being a tenant farmer for Mr. Arvis Cagley would be far worse than being dead. Finding a pocketful of pearls was Obie's only hope of paying off the taxes and his daddy's debt to Mr. Arvis Cagley.

Obie's gaze followed the river upstream until it

turned and a wall of trees broke his view. There, and towering above the river, stood an outcropping of rock that resembled a castle. Its shadow fell across the water and stood like a sentinel against a morning sky on fire. Slanted slivers of color knifed through the trees to mix with the muted overcast that hung above the dark water. Obie raised his face to the dampness in hopes of being blessed by its beauty.

Six days had passed since leaving Wilks Hollow. Six days, when he figured to take only three. They had been lucky at first, caught a ride right off with a man hauling hard sugar maples. Then the rains began and everything turned sour.

Obie looked toward the high knob. From up there, he would be able to see far enough east to pick out the place where the Yuda and Sallapoosa joined. Would the mussel beds be there?

Obie glanced over his shoulder. He watched Bas poke at the fire. It seemed that the only real friends Obie had were Josh, Mrs. Middleton and Chaser. His little brother and the schoolteacher were too far off for talking and Chaser would follow him anywhere, even if it was a no-account idea. Could he talk to Bas? Could he trust his brother's friend?

Not likely. Bas and Virg went hunting together. They chewed tobacco and drank Sarson Allardice's moonshine. Bas had only asked to come along because—

Obie chose not to remember the reason and shut out the thoughts before they took root. "Durn river," he muttered, "mussels are more scarce than snake feathers." And he circled the end of his line around a grayback and started back to the fire.

Across the river and standing inside a gray-green haze rose the black and disfigured arms of dead chestnuts. Buzzards perched there. They watched him; he felt their intense beady eyes. Did they sense his fate, sense that he, too, would eventually face the same end as those who preceded him to the mussel beds? Did they have their minds set on which parts of him they would eat?

"Durn you!" he yelled, and grabbed a rock. He threw it as far as he could, and as high, but once the arc broke, the rock dropped into the river's murky water.

He looked up and caught Bas watching. "If you want to go home, then get," Obie shouted. "I didn't ask you to come along, and I'll not ask you to stay. I'll manage fine on my own!"

Obie poured steaming coffee into a tin cup. Without thinking he pressed both hands around it, yelled from the sudden pain, dropped it immediately while dancing around on one foot and blowing on his palms.

Everything was wrong. Nothing was going right and he kicked dirt into the fire.

"Rub this into your skin. Won't smart for more than a minute." Bas handed Obie an oily cloth from his tow sack. "It's bear's grease."

Bas sat back beside the fire, eyed Obie in a thoughtful way. "Heared your daddy say that you was short on patience, had a heap too much pride for your size and you'd fight a circle saw if you took a mind to. Reckon he knowd you good."

Bas picked up the tin cup, cleaned the sand from inside and refilled it. "Coffee's some better," he said. "Ain't near as nasty tasting as last evening." He turned the handle toward Obie. "Ain't gonna lie to you, turkey-

23

tailing it for home has crossed my mind but I give my word."

Bas raised his own cup to his lips and looked over the rim. "Ain't gonna lie about being skeered last night neither. This here place and that story your daddy told, ever' time he come to Felker Mountain, gives me the crawlies. Makes me mad that I can't pick out what's true from what's storytelling."

Bas sucked up the hot coffee cautiously. "I got no belly for going deeper into River Country but I knowd what finding them pearls means to you. 'Pears to me that this here river is too durn high and moving too fast for what you're wanting to do. Might be though, that the Yuda's gonna be some better. And since you ain't gonna give this up until you see for yourself, I say we pack up and get before something happens to change my mind."

It was the longest speech Obie had ever heard an Allardice make. It surprised him, too, that Bas knew so many words. "I'm grateful," Obie said, "and it's not just for me that I need to find the pearls. If I go home with nothing, Mr. Arvis Cagley will take our land and make tenant farmers of us Wilkses."

Obie peered into the cup of hot, black coffee. "Virg and Orvull will light out soon as that happens; they got no strong feelings for mamma or the younguns, and I can't work eighty acres of tableland by myself."

After sipping the coffee, he added, "Mr. Arvis Cagley will throw us off our land if we can't work it, same as he did the Swoforths up Brandy Creek way. County people will send the younguns to the orphans' home and Mamma to the poor farm."

Obie whistled for Chaser, watched her lope across

the sand toward him. "I don't know of another way to help my family, Bas."

Chaser licked the side of Obie's face, lay down beside him and rested her chin on his knee. Her tired and sorrowful brown eyes told him that she understood.

CHAPTER

3

* * *

OBIE PICKED HIS WAY TO THE HIGHEST PLACE ON THE KNOB and looked out over a symmetrical quiescence of peaks and ridges. How different it appeared in daylight. Hazy, he thought, like everything wrapped inside of a cocoon. Yet the uninterrupted mantle of multicolored vegetation concealed the landmarks he sought. The mountains lay southwest to northeast and were separated by valleys and hollows, an occasional cove. Obie followed the course of the Sallapoosa that lay below. But soon the forest obstructed his view. He studied the lay of the trees on both sides of the valley, hoping for a clue that might suggest where the Yuda joined the Sallapoosa. "The place those two rivers meet is down there," Obie said. "You have any idea how far east it might be?"

"Mebbe there."

Obie considered the direction Bas pointed. On both sides of the valley, mountains lay like unbroken chains.

But a dividing ridge between the two unbroken ranges ended at the valley's far eastern edge. Could Bas be right?

"If we hug this here ridge, we're sure to find a place for a better look." Bas hoisted his rifle and tow sack. "And keep your eyes skinned. Don't want nothing coming on us sudden like."

Obie hurried down from the knob, turned east. Without a path to follow, he picked his way slowly along the mountain's southerly slope. He kept to the high side of the limestone ledge while shallow caves broke the wall of layered rock that rose on his left. Obie welcomed the warmth that burned through the haze. It reached down between the trees to heat the air and earth.

They stopped at a spring and drank their fill while Chaser stretched her long body flat in the clear pool. They heard birds but could not see the singers. They saw shadows dart around and above them. To hear and see the evidence of creatures so close yet miss the tangible signs left Obie with an unsettling sensation that worked its way into his mind. "Come on," he said, "let's get shed of this place."

The incline continued to rise through a hillside of pine trees, mountain laurel and dog-hobble. Obie continually searched for a knob or protruding ledge that would allow him a view of the valley floor. But always, he looked over the same tangled confusion of thickets and trees. Finally he suggested that they leave high ground and make their way down. "I know we'll find where those two rivers join up. I know it."

"Ain't gonna be easy going through that brush-thicket. Worse than this here," Bas said. "But I reckon you got your mind set."

"I know the Yuda flows into the Sallapoosa from the south. That means we'll have to cross the Sallapoosa," Obie said. "Keep mindful for a place, will you?"

Once again Obie took the lead. He noticed Bas grimace and suspected that crossing the river disturbed him. It bothered Obie, too. Every step of their descent took them deeper into a country that had made his great-granddaddy say, *"Few white men ever live to tell what they seen in that wilderness."*

As the ground leveled, tall trees formed a canopy that compressed the sunlight into an enclosure of shadows and diffused light. A great stillness surrounded them. Mountains on both sides towered overhead like watchful sentries, poised there to warn of any outsider's passage into the forbidden regions. It was impossible to observe them without feeling the quiet terror of their silent strength. Obie reached for Chaser. "You stay with me," he said, aware of the growing temptation to retreat.

The Yuda was out there; he heard it, a swirling, distant eddy moving with slithering quiet. An impulse suggested to Obie that he run. But where? Forest blanketed the hillside, covered the valley floor and up the other side. Below him an umbrella of trees, an almost impenetrable head-high snarl of vines and briars forced him to his knees, to crawl and kick his way through.

"This here blackberry-hell can tear a fellow's shirt clean off his back," Bas said.

"You can take the lead if it would be easier," Obie called back. "Just keep a close watch on Chaser."

"No need. You're doing fine."

Bas lived in a hollow up Felker Mountain. His daddy and brothers taught him to use a rifle before he grew big enough to carry one. He took part in all their hunting adventures—the tracking, the stalking, the killing, the skinning, the butchering, the eating. Bas had a sharp eye, a keen sense and good knowledge of where wild creatures hid and their other habits. Obie could only guess why Bas chose now to hang back instead of taking the lead.

Besides skunk and bobcat, bear and wild boar fed on wild berries, acorns and nuts, which were everywhere. True, those devils were busy filling their bellies in the fall season. True, they would light out if they caught a man's scent, but if they were downwind and come upon sudden, they would charge. And in such a thicket, Obie knew there would be no escape.

He shivered. His lungs labored to take in, then let out the heavy afternoon air. A tightness pressed against his chest while a dryness in his throat cut like a knife. He tried to move faster but the dense vegetation and lichen-covered graybacks routed him in a zigzag course, and he wondered: Was Bas's decision to hang back a deliberate choice? Obie twisted and side-stepped his way ahead, realizing suddenly that it was not only the four-legged creatures he should be concerned about. The damp beech bottom, which they were crossing, was home for copperheads, a stray cottonmouth maybe, and any number of other poisonous creatures.

Obie swore under his breath; how far was that dang river? He heard it; the roar near deafened him now. Obie called back over his shoulder, "It can't be much farther. Seems like we've traveled the whole blessed day."

When Bas failed to respond, Obie wrenched around. A fleeting glimpse of Bas's broad shoulders stilled the sudden panic that swept through him. "How come you didn't answer?" he shouted. "You deaf or something?"

"I didn't know you was asking."

29

Obie clenched his teeth. Dumb hillbilly! Every Allardice there was should be operated on for the simples. The sudden anger propelled him ahead with about as much concern for Bas and the branches that whipped back as a bear would have for a swarm of bees.

Except for the increasing noise, Obie came upon the Sallapoosa without warning. Boulders, big as bears and polished smooth by centuries of wet buffeting, broken logs, stumps and their spiderlike legs clutching bits of hide and moss jumbled together on the river's deep and churning outside curve.

Obie hesitated. If he took to thinking and planned his way across, he knew his courage would vanish. "Let's cross right here," Obie yelled and whistled for Chaser to follow. "We'll not find a more likely spot."

Obie leaped from the bank to the nearest grayback. His foot slipped on the wet surface. It threw him off balance as he jumped to the next boulder. One foot went into the river but his knee struck the edge of the rock and saved him from falling in. He pulled himself up. He took short steps, then vaulted from one granite boulder to the next, walking heel-to-toe along partially submerged logs, crawling his way over the gnarled roots of bobbing stumps. Once he reached the gravel bar in the center, he fought the impulse to stop and rest. "Chaser," he yelled, "come on, girl." Then he ran ahead without turning to see if she was following.

He raced the length of the gravel bar before he jumped. He landed in knee-deep water and felt the immediate pull of the current. He struggled forward, stumbling sometimes, always stretching toward the field of fragmented rocks along the river's shallow south side.

Out of breath and grabbing for a handful of switch cane, Obie drew himself out of the water. Chaser followed and shook herself. "Damn," Bas exclaimed and collapsed on the wide reach of beargrass beside Obie. "You got no more sense than a feist that thinks he's a bear dog."

Muscles quivered in Obie's legs and a spinning sickness made him hang his head. Sweat trickled down his spine. Everything turned. He spun back to the river, fell face down in the cold water. He was going to throw up all right, but not so his brother's friend could see.

CHAPTER

4

✳ ✳ ✳

SLOWLY OBIE TURNED FROM THE FIRE AND THREW THE apple core into the woods. His gaze met Bas's. "Durned if you ain't a puzzle," Bas said. "You could have got yourself kilt crossing that river the way you done."

"How come you followed me?"

Bas pursed his lips and finally shrugged. "I ain't good stringing words together but I followed you for the same reason that brung me." Bas glanced over his shoulder. "This here looks to be a likely spot for spending the night."

While using the sleeve of his shirt to polish his rifle barrel, Bas added, "If we keep on a-walking, we ain't apt to have fresh meat for supper."

"Sounds good to me; I'm empty as a dry well." And Obie ran his hand across his belly. "Think I'll follow the shallows upstream. Maybe I'll get lucky and stumble onto the crossing of the two rivers."

"Too bad that map you got ain't more exacting." Bas shouldered his rifle. "Until I get the lay of these here hills, you best keep a hold on Chaser. Don't want her tearing off on no scent and me having to chase after."

Bas moved southeast and disappeared into the woods. The sound of his steps faded almost immediately and Obie pulled the rope from his tow sack. He made Chaser a collar and tied her to a nearby chestnut tree. "Don't want you running after me either, you hear?"

She whined and jerked on the rope before settling near the fire. Resting her chin on her paws, Chaser watched Obie slip from his overalls, his shoes and socks.

He stepped into the water. Rocks, small and fragmented, pierced his bare feet; the water's cold made goose bumps up his bare legs and turned the skin blue. He moved farther along the shallow edge, crouched and raked his fingers across the bottom for pigtoes. Instead, he dredged up small chunks of granite, feldspar and flint rock. Was he mistaken in trusting the map and all the old stories? Was he a fool like his brother thought, a dreamer?

Obie continued upstream. He continued to search the murky water for those telltale trails that mussels left along the bottom. He searched until wide shadows darkened the water even more.

Obie debated about going farther. He considered the time; it was getting on, all right. The thought of making his way back in the dark persuaded him, yet he eyed the next bend, the butt-end of a ridge, only partially visible from where he stood. Could that be the place where the rivers joined? Could the mussel beds that Micager told about be just around the next stand of trees? Should he go a short ways more? Curiosity tempted him. Thunder . . . ? Obie raised his face to the sky. Patches of hazy blue showed through the overhead canopy of limbs and leaves. Was it thunder or had he heard Bas's rifle?

The thought of feasting on venison liver rather than mush propelled Obie back along the shallow edge of the Sallapoosa. It suddenly seemed unimportant that he had not discovered a pigtoe bed or found evidence of one. Tomorrow. He planned ahead as he jogged to the clearing and his dog.

Chaser whined. She jumped and jerked against the rope. Obie hugged her as he unloosened the rope from around her neck. A breeze off the river hurried him into his overalls and he reached deep into his pockets for the map and quarters to satisfy the fear of losing them. "Thank you, Lord," he muttered, as he moved about the edge of the forest gathering wood.

He rebuilt the fire, filled the pot with water from a nearby spring. Tomorrow, he kept telling himself, tomorrow he would find where the rivers joined. He boiled coffee, sliced bacon, stirred up a batter of cornmeal, salt and water for cooking in the hot fat. He was hungrier than a she-bear with cubs.

Obie settled himself near the fire and poked at the coals. The wind and its growing chill brought to mind the November first due date on his daddy's note to Mr. Arvis Cagley, who was definitely not the sort to permit tardiness. He wanted Wilks Hollow and would snap it up faster than a cottonmouth could strike.

Obie removed his great-granddaddy's map and carefully smoothed it over the knee of his patched overalls. He followed the line of the river he had spent the afternoon searching. A mile or so ahead of where he had stopped, he remembered seeing the butt-end of a rocky ridge. Obie matched that with a large X on Micager's map. Was that the place the rivers joined? A line squiggled up the right hand side of the paper. Was that the Yuda? If it was, then it had to be no more than a mile ahead. "A mile?" Obie questioned, and drew back his shoulders.

If that line was the Yuda, then the other half-dozen wiggly marks flowing off to the south had to represent creeks and branches. "Yeah!" Obie shouted. It was going to happen; he wasn't a fool, a dreamer either. And it was no "pie-in-the-sky" kind of notion like his mamma said. Virg and Orvull . . . well, they could take to sleeping with one eye open if they ever had the urge to laugh at him again.

"Tomorrow." Obie laughed. "Tomorrow." And he looked back at the map, wondering which one of those half-dozen wiggly lines held the mussel beds.

Rather than being discouraged by the map's lack of details, Obie bounced up from his place beside the fire. He cleared rocks from the ground where he intended to lay his pallet. He cleared a larger square for Bas, then gathered armloads of crisp leaves and cut fronds from the spicy smelling ferns. They would make a softer and drier bed than the damp earth.

Before darkness settled in, Bas returned with four squirrels thrown over his shoulder and a bib full of wild sweet potatoes. Though Obie had never heard of them growing wild, the excitement of finding where the two rivers joined pushed that detail from his mind. "I do believe, clean to my soul, that this here map is right, right to the wee-tiniest detail."

Bas shrugged. He held the squirrels up for Obie to

see. "Told you I was good. Got these little fellers with just one shot."

"One bullet? You're a lying storyteller. But you come on it honest. Your daddy were the windiest man I ever—"

"My daddy?" Chaser stood next to Bas at the river while he skinned and gutted the squirrels. "He weren't never the hair-raisingest liar your daddy were. To this here day I still dream about that old witch Dalton swore hung around Claiborne Wilks's burnt-out cabin. That were the God-awfulest story I ever heard a man tell."

Obie poked at the glowing embers. He pictured his daddy, tall and lanky, whiskered, black hair hanging on his neck, weaving another of his tales. Dalton Wilks loved storytelling. After a gulp or two of Sarson's moonshine there was not a better yarn-spinner living. But his daddy swore, swore on the Good Book, that the witch inside his daddy Claiborne's burnt-out cabin was truth, not something from his imagination.

The fire died down until the embers satisfied Bas for roasting meat. He slid a long stick through the ribs of each squirrel but it was Obie who took the first turn and rotated the meat slowly above the coals.

As it cooked, juices dripped into the fire. Flames blazed up and the odor brought Chaser close to Obie's side. She stretched flat, slapped her tail back and forth, whined. There would not be much else for her than bones and scraps, yet she licked her chops as if expecting it all.

"Smells belly-wrenching good." Bas propped himself against a tree. "It rattle you that you didn't come on no mussels?"

"Some," Obie answered, "but there's something bothering me more."

While Bas fingered the square tear in his overalls, Obie went on: "When we were making our way down here this morning, we could have come across a bear in that thicket, maybe a bobcat. Been no way that I could have gotten out of its path. Guess what I'm wondering is how come you to stick me out in front, you being the hunter and all."

Bas drew his mouth to one side while picking at the tear in his overalls. "Is it just me that you don't trust, Obie, or is it everyone?"

Obie continued to turn the meat. "Before I answer your question, I'd like you to answer mine."

The brim of Bas's hat shaded his forehead and eyes, concealed whatever silent response prompted him to nod in a slow, deliberate motion. "I'm some taller than you," he said. "Stick me in front and all them stickery switches would have come whipping back at you. Cut your face raw, tore your duds worse than they did mine."

Bas unfolded his arms, opened them to show the rips in his shirt. " 'Sides that," he went on, "don't take a heap of smarts to know that all you got to do is call out, drop down and give me room to shoot."

Obie turned his head but not his eyes and observed the way Bas sat there, relaxed, chewing on a blade of beargrass, waiting. Obie felt obliged to respond; an apology was needed. Instead, he questioned his own mistrust. Was it because Bas was Virg's friend? Was it just Virg's friends that he mistrusted or everyone? He trusted his daddy but Dalton Wilks went and got himself killed; trusted his mamma but now it seemed that she thought more about herself and the younguns than him. Being the oldest son carried more responsibilities than being a mother cat.

Obie blinked as Bas rose to his knees and crawled to the fire. He pressed his finger to the hot, juicy meat, then to his tongue. "Tasty good," he said, and poured coffee. "While I were hunting I come on a cove no bigger than pocket size. Seen signs of a cabin and cleared ground. Besides finding the sweet potatoes, which I've never known to grow wild, I found this."

Bas reached into his pocket. He withdrew his hand and unfolded it slowly. "You know, don't you, that this here is Indian."

Obie studied it carefully. "What is it?"

"It's the bowl to a pipe . . . smoking pipe. Soapstone, and that carving right there is the face of an owl. My gran'daddy had one years back, excepting his was carved with the face of a Cherokee."

"Are you telling me that you think there are still Indians living in these mountains?"

"I'm telling you this here is Indian. It didn't walk in here all by its lonesome and somebody planted them sweet-taters."

Obie fed the fire with twigs to keep the flame from dying. He supposed that years ago men, Indian or otherwise, could have moved so deep into the mountains that they would never have been found unless they had chosen to be. It could have happened, and Obie looked off into the nighttime sky wondering if a lone survivor remained out there. Finally he asked, "Anything else back there?"

"Lots of deer and wild boar signs. Both make good eats."

"This cove, is it far?"

Bas took his turn and rotated the spit. "Just a little piece."

"Did you see a river?"

After Bas nodded, Obie said, "I bet it's the Yuda." He unfolded the map and explained to Bas the meaning of the lines. "Come sunup we'll head off that way."

"Mebbe you ought to roast them sweet-taters in the coals. They'll be tasty tomorrow."

Obie agreed and afterward fried bacon and cooked corn cakes in the hot grease until the edges turned golden lacy. Obie ate his plain but Bas poured molasses over his. He sucked the squirrel bones clean before throwing them to Chaser. But Obie left scraps of meat and fed her corn cakes from his plate.

While Bas cleaned his rifle, Obie scoured the skillet with a handful of gravel, then repacked the tow sack except for the pot to boil morning coffee.

"You judge that tale about your great-gran'daddy coming here is more story talk than truth?"

"Not on your life! He did come here and he did find a pearl. Something happened to him, too, something that scared him spitless."

Bas pursed his lips before drawing the rifle to his shoulder. He stared down the barrel. "What about the stone man?" He rested the rifle across his legs. "That gospel truth?"

Obie divided the dried leaves and fern fronds. He wrapped up in his quilt before stretching out on his stomach, facing the fire. "That was storytelling. My daddy and gran'daddy always added and changed to make a tale better."

Bas leaned forward. "You know how to shoot this here rifle, don't you?"

"I've fired one a time or two."

Bas studied him with a raised eyebrow before saying, "I reckon we'll both do more sleeping if we take turns staying awake. I'll watch first."

"I don't mind," Obie volunteered.

But Bas shook off the offer. "If I shut my eyes now my head is gonna be wondering if your eyes is open. If I set up until my head turns fuzzy like, then I'll drop off real easy."

Obie rolled onto his back. He tucked one arm under Chaser and the other beneath his head. A million stars lit the sky and Obie picked out the Big Dipper. He took a deep breath, closed both eyes. The sounds of fire and river faded until they were no longer sounds.

He dropped off expecting to be awakened in a few hours but when he opened his eyes, gray light and a foggy veil hung above the river. It filled every crack of open space. He sat upright, looked in all directions, listened.

The fire had burnt out; Bas, curled in a heap, snored loudly and Chaser slept beside him. He shook Bas's shoulder before going to the river and dipping his face into the cold water. He shivered, smoothed back his hair and returned to the fire with an armload of wood. "Thought we were going to take turns staying awake."

Bas scratched his head. "You riled at me for nodding off?"

"I have no reason to be sore." Obie hesitated. "I'm sorry about last night, about thinking that you hung back to save yourself. I was wrong and I apologize." Obie added new wood to last night's coals. "Sometimes I get so busy thinking about the way things look to be that I forget to see all that's going on."

They ate hot mush with molasses, sweet potatoes

and drank coffee before they shouldered the tow sacks and set off. Obie figured to follow the Sallapoosa until reaching the Yuda but Bas took the lead and headed southeast.

They pushed, climbed and crawled their way through thickets of dog-hobble and spicebush, plum and sumac. What Bas said about the stickery switches was true and Obie used his tow sack as a shield to protect his face.

Twice Bas paused long enough to point out deep slash marks on the buckeyes, made there years ago by axmen who once hacked out a narrow trail across the mountains. As the slope rose, the vegetation changed. "Don't that look like a trail that's been used, and used recent?" Bas asked, then pointed ahead to a ribbon of ground that dipped in the center. Wood sorrel grew on both sides. Witch hazel, too. And the sun burned through the damp gray coverlet to warm the corridor of hard-packed earth.

Obviously it was a passageway, as Bas suspicioned. Had Cherokees once used it? Did someone use it still? Fresh droppings indicated that deer used the trail and the boys followed it higher, moving parallel along the mountain's northerly slope.

When Bas stopped a second time, he pointed down into a cove that he had seen the day before. Was it simply an old beaver meadow or had the land been cleared? Numerous tree stumps ringed the clearing of beargrass and switch cane. Had the labor been done by Cherokees?

Obie reached down and ran his hand the length of Chaser's spine. Ninety years ago, one thousand full-blooded Cherokees broke from the remainder of what had once been a powerful and civilized nation. They refused to follow their brothers and the government's request that they move west onto a reservation. Instead, they fled into the mountains and disappeared. Were they, and all of their children, dead now? Were there any survivors? If there were, were they living out their lives hidden away in a wilderness that stretched across into North Carolina? Obie could only guess as he started down to the river.

"Hold up." Bas rested a hand on Obie's shoulder. "Got something more to show you."

Obie followed Bas over rocks, through bushes and around ledges that jutted out above slides of milky white quartz. Deep crevices and man-sized indentations broke the sheer vertical wall. Bas stopped. He bent down and drank from a spring that bubbled out of a broad fissure. The clear water tasted cool and sweet. It filled a shallow, scooped-out rock, then fell off and disappeared down a sink. "See over there." Bas pointed ahead. "I came on that cave yesterday. Ain't very deep but it's a sight better than sleeping down by the river."

Obie crawled inside. He felt a continual draft, heard the dripping trickle of water. He set his tow sack aside, studying the scabby rock walls. Deeper back he recognized stalactites and moss-covered stalagmites. Had Indians once taken refuge in this cave? Had one of them lived out a winter here? Near the entrance soot blackened the cave's walls and ceiling. A red man's fire or someone else's? Obie crawled back outside and helped Bas build a fire on the ledge. They would be safe here from whatever two- or four-legged critters prowled the night, and dry if it rained. Obie emptied his tow sack; Bas did the same. While he sorted through the remainder of their food supply, Obie stuffed two gunnysacks that he had carried from home inside the bib of his overalls and coiled the grappling rope around his shoulder.

"You want me to help with the pearling or fix up for night?"

"Fix up," Obie answered and looked down toward the river. Streaks of frothy white ripples showed on the surface. Graybacks littered both sides of the stream bed, some big as automobiles. On the other side buckeye and maples grew along the narrow ribbon of flat bottom. Rising up toward the ridge, oak and hickories shared the hillside with graybacks, mountain laurel and all sorts of other bushes and briars. But below where he now stood on the ledge, he saw those same deep slash marks carved into the few leafless chestnuts left standing. As Obie moved down from the ledge, he noticed that the slash marks were crudely shaped figures of men, which added to the probability that Indians once lived in what now remained of a log cabin at the far-back edge of the cove.

But it was the sudden thought of finding pearls that sent him across the grassy bottom. Clouds passed in front of the sun and left a damp chill. Would it rain or had the threat passed? He dismissed that, too, and stood gazing into the river.

The Yuda was smaller than the Sallapoosa, less cluttered with debris and less muddy. Rivers spoke with their own voices, he remembered his granddaddy telling him. *"Some wear gentle faces, others look mean, cussed-ornery, but they'll tell a feller all sorts of secrets, like how old they is."* Obie studied the shallow apron, the tiny eddies that whirled and washed sand from beneath larger rocks. Toward the center an occasional boulder reached up from the dark and deep channel that flowed fast and silent.

Obie stepped back from the edge, wondering

43

whether it would be wiser to wade out and search the bottom with his hands and bare feet or use the grappling line. Something unseen and unheard made him glance over his shoulder and study the remains of the old log cabin. Shadows and haze bathed it in smoky light. Was there something truly spooky about River Country or was his uneasiness simply the result of having heard too many tales?

Obie shook the coil of rope from his shoulder. He chose a rock and tied it to the grappling line for added weight before throwing it toward the center. The rock hit. An eruption of water shot skyward, and he felt the immediate pull as the stone settled to the bottom.

Picking his way carefully along the rocky apron, Obie moved downstream and drew the line behind him. Visions of pearls replaced his uneasiness. They projected pictures in his brain of mussel beds and pearls as big as marbles. His head swelled with impatience. He wished he could tell his daddy, his granddaddy and Micager Wilks that he had found the place. He wished he could get word to his mamma that everything was going fine.

Satisfied that he had gone far enough and noticing that the river dropped off a few yards farther ahead, Obie backed toward the bank and drew the rope after him. He was not positive but the line felt cumbersome, heavier. Finally, with his feet planted on solid ground, he began to pull on the rope.

"Jiminie, criminie! Bas," Obie yelled. "I found them. I found them, Bas!"

Lord-a-mighty . . . the whole line was heavy with pigtoes.

CHAPTER
5
* * *

BY NIGHTFALL A VARIETY OF MUSSELS LAY ON THE ROCKY ledge where Bas had dumped them. Sounds from the river and animals, beginning their nocturnal search, drifted upward to mix with the sweet hickory scented smoke from Bas's fire. Turnip chunks and bacon cooked inside the kettle. Chaser, stretched between the fire and the cave's entrance, watched Obie stare at the nubby and rough-textured blackish gray mussel in his hand. "Go on," Bas said, "slit it open."

Resting on his knees, Obie curled his fingers around the pigtoe. He raised the knife, directed the point toward that seam between the two shells. But the mussel resisted with the resolve of an impenetrable fortress.

"That shore is a contrary thing," Bas said.

Obie bit his lower lip and repositioned the blade, using it like a lever, raising one side then the other, always pushing forward. At last the piercing point pricked some inner nerve. A vibrating spasm relaxed the tension and unlocked the fortress. Obie cast off the top shell. He held the remains close to the fire and used the point of the knife to lay apart the folds of gray-white flesh. But there was no sign of a pearl. Disappointment rushed the length of his body. Without a word, he flipped the meat into the kettle and reached for another.

There was no patience now, no inner ceremony of praying or holding his lips a certain way. Only the angry force of an unsatisfied desire remained; he had so little and wanted so much. Obie drove the knife blade between the shells. He twisted and pried and jabbed until the tension ceased, then flung aside the upper portion.

"Lawdy," Bas whispered. "Lookie there."

Obie pushed his hand closer toward the fire, moved the pigtoe until it caught the best light. He blinked. Was it true? Had he really found his first pearl?

It loomed up at him, wet and slick looking, its shimmers of pastel colors enhanced by the firelight. Along with a slow, deep-throated sigh, Obie said, "Ain't it near the most beautiful thing you ever saw?"

He focused all of his attention on the pearl. An excited swelling slowly stirred inside his chest. It bubbled and churned until he finally yelled, "We did it, Bas! We did it."

Chaser jumped up from her place near the cave's entrance, whirled around in search of the varmint that caused the explosion in her master's voice. Obie laughed, drew his dog down beside him. "We're gonna find ourselves a sack full of these before we go home. A whole sack full."

The pearl Obie lifted from inside the shell was rectangular, irregular rather than smooth. Bas asked, "You ever seen one of them round ones that comes from the ocean?"

"Seen pictures," Obie replied. "You know why those are round while fresh water pearls look all whomper-jawed?"

Bas stuck a twig between his teeth and shook his head. "Well," Obie began, "ocean pearls are round and smooth because of the back and forth motion of ocean tides. You want to hold it?"

Bas sucked in his cheeks. "I figured you was tetched when Virg told me you was going pearling. I laughed right along with your brothers; none of us figured you knew beans with the bag open." Bas rolled the pearl between his thumb and forefinger. "It's shore a puny, wee-little thing."

Little? It was big as a mountain. Then Obie saw it with his eyes and not his heart. Bas handed it back. "You're right," Obie said, "it's not very big but larger than a seed pearl. One of those weighs less than a quarter of a pearl grain. That's the size they use to make necklaces."

"Them the smallest kind?"

Obie shook his head and picked up another mussel. "There are dust pearls; they're no bigger than a half-second."

He pried the shells apart. He examined the flesh, then shrugged and tossed it into the pot. "How come you to know so much about pearls?" Bas asked.

"Learned it from books."

"Them books tell you where to sell these play-pretties?"

"No, but Mrs. Middleton did. There's a man in Nashville—"

"How come her to know?"

"Her mamma grew up in the Cumberland; she's got kin living in those parts. Claiworthy's their name."

Bas turned his head and looked from beneath a raised brow.

"It's true," Obie defended. "The man that's going to buy our pearls is Mr. Aaron Smith. That is if we get home in time to take them there. I'll trade them for dollars unless you want to keep your half." Obie added another mussel to the kettle. "I'm going to pay off my daddy's debt, the taxes owed on our land, then I'm going to—"

"Hot-dang!" Bas exclaimed. "There's another."

They each took turns holding it, before Bas placed it on the tow sack beside the first one. "How you figure a pearl gets itself inside them shells?"

"It grows there." Obie continued to reach for, open, then discard. "The mussel, when it's feeding off the bottom, sucks up something sharp, like a piece of sand or a sliver of rock that gets stuck between its shell and mantle."

"Mantle? What's that?"

Obie held up the meaty part of one of the mussels, which they were going to cook. "To stop that piece of grit from hurting, the mussel squirts a brown, sticky liquid all over it. That's called *nacre.*" Obie stretched a hand out. "Nacre is this stuff on my fingers and the mussel continues to squirt nacre on that piece of grit time after time."

"You telling me that pearls is layered like onions?"

"I suppose that's true, except you can't see the layers."

48

"Obie . . ." Bas shook his head. "I do believe you found another."

Bas bent forward for a closer look. "What ails it? Pearls ain't supposed to be flat, is they?"

Obie lifted the pearl from the white sticky flesh. "This is called a button pearl. Somehow the piece of grit that this mussel picked up stuck to the inside of its shell and only got nacre sprayed on the one side. That's why this side is flat and the other more rounded. This is the kind that's used for making rings."

"There other kinds?"

Obie continued adding meat to the kettle and explained: "A little bug can find its way into the shell. The mussel spews nacre over it the same as it would a piece of grit. That kind of pearl is called a blister."

"Does that hole where the bug was ever fill up?"

"Don't think so. There's just one other kind of pearl that I know about and it's called a baroque. Well," he said, kicking the empty shells from the ledge, "three are better than none but tomorrow I have to do better." He wiped his hands down the legs of his overalls before wrapping the three pearls inside the toe of a clean sock.

Bas poured the watery stew into tin cups. He tasted his cautiously. "That's as gritty-tasted as I ever ate," he said. "You got to swaller it fast."

"Tomorrow," Obie said, "I'll work the river down below, then move upstream, work my way southeast."

Smoke flavored the stew and Obie swallowed it quickly, keeping his mind on tomorrow rather than what was going into his belly. "You can come along if you want, but if you don't, that's okay, too."

Bas rolled the cup between his hands. "Ain't that I'm not willing to help, Obie, it's just that I'd like to shoot myself a wild pig. There's a mess of sign and we're getting low on food."

"There's meal and bacon, apples and shuck beans. We'll not starve."

"Ain't nothing you mentioned gonna fill my belly for very long." Bas wrinkled his nose. "Can't say that I'm fond of this here stew." Bas raised his face to the sky. "Night's turned a might airish; could rain before sunup."

Obie built up the fire with wood Bas had gathered during the afternoon. While Bas talked about tracking a wild boar, Obie thought about finding pearls, about the changes they would bring to his life. Soon as the family's debts were settled, his mamma taken care of, he was heading north. His uncle Tully lived in Michigan and Obie intended to go there. He would need advice about making his own way. He knew that logging, like his daddy had done, or working the mines in Kentucky, like his mamma's brothers had done, had no appeal to him. But helping build automobiles alongside his uncle Tully seemed like an exciting thing to do.

Obie moved inside the cave. He stretched flat on the pallet of evergreen boughs and dried needles, closed his eyes and soon drifted off. He slept deeply for hours, then began to thrash about and mutter incoherently.

Faces without bodies rose from the thick mist and passed before him. The faces were not angry or grotesque ones, rather familiar faces of people yet unknown—some smiling, some thin-lipped, some hollow-eyed, some soulful. They moved in single file as if there to inspect him and judge for themselves. They passed so quietly that he heard a copperhead slither through the grass. The last face had no features but had arms and legs and a doeskin over its head. An arm reached out to him—an arm without hand or fingers, offering a cup filled with pearls. They glittered like a distant galaxy. Obie reached for the cup but it was withdrawn, then offered again but held inches beyond his grasp. He ran after it, followed it from the mountains, over rivers and hills, beyond home. He chased after it until everything grew strange. Even the hand he reached out changed . . . bony, bent, clawlike, twisted. Obie drew back. He shook his arm to rid himself of the hand. But it remained. He tucked it behind his back so no one would see; he jammed it into his pocket, not wanting to think about it. But every place the hand touched, decay set in. "No," Obie yelled, and ran from the horror. He ran until his lungs stung and threatened to explode. He ran. . . .

Obie tossed back and forth on the pallet of pine-scented boughs. He muttered words without understanding the sounds. He shook his head until the feel of something cold and wet came between his mind and the dream.

Obie ran his hand over his forehead. Water continued to drip from a crevice in the rock ceiling. He sat up, shivered and brought his hands close to his face. Night, and the dark cave kept him from knowing. But they felt the same; they smelled of smoke and mussels. He wiggled his fingers, watched them move back and forth.

He drew his knees against his chest and held them inside both arms. A dream, but what did it mean? He chewed on his lip. A dream, just a dream, a silly dream. Rather than lying back, closing his eyes and drifting off again, he took one deep breath after another.

He blamed Bas's stew for the dream, cold river water for the chills. He wrapped himself in his mamma's old quilt and crawled out onto the ledge. He rebuilt the fire, huddled close to the warmth while watching dawn creep over the eastern rim. Finally Bas stirred.

Obie chose not to discuss his dream with Bas. Instead he talked about trailing alongside the Yuda until he came on the first branch, then following it. "No way that I can get myself lost," he said. "I'll just keep to one branch at a time, then when I've worked it, I'll head back to the Yuda."

When he left the ledge, he took along his grappling line, knife, hatchet, three apples to hold him through the day and Bas's sharpening stone. He threw the tow sack over his shoulder and called for Chaser, then ran across the bottom to the river. He paused there for a moment to look at the boulders, at the fast moving water churning and falling around the rocks, at the dark and mysterious trough down the center. There were mussels in there all right, but the number of pearls he had found the night before disappointed him, and he struck off upstream.

The river took one turn after another and Obie kept close to the edge, always looking for a track across the sandy bottom. Several times he waded out to pick up a mussel but none possessed a pearl and he moved on.

As the ground continued to rise, the river changed. Water plunged over an upper ledge, around sheer-faced walls into huge graybacks that diverted its direction again. It churned and foamed and roared until the sound of it filled Obie with its overpowering presence. He sensed its strength, its unwillingness to relinquish its treasures. But he had traveled too far to be intimidated by a roaring river and he continued over the rise.

Again the river changed to a broad stretch of lazy water that passed beneath a shelter of oak and hickories.

Slivers of morning light pierced through the loose weave of branches and leaves to mottle the river's gray-green surface. It looked promising and he considered using the grappling line. But trees and a mass of undergrowth pushed into the river's shallow edge.

"Chaser," Obie called, "come back here before you get yourself lost."

He studied the river again. From one of Mrs. Middleton's books, he'd read about men pearling from a scow and using a crowfoot drag on the big rivers. He would have to give it some thought but he was confident that with Bas's help he could build a similar contraption. The possibilities excited him. He considered turning back, finding Bas and asking for his help. But Bas would be hunting. "Come on, Chaser—" Obie slapped his leg "—let's look up ahead."

Trees and thickets of rhododendron, fern and vine crowded the bank. The dense mass forced Obie to his knees, to push the tow sack ahead and use it like a ram while Chaser bellied her way behind. In some places the growth took on a deeper color. Its primitive look suggested that nothing human had passed through this wilderness for hundreds of years. And Obie crawled faster until he came upon a branch that flowed into the Yuda from the southeast.

Resting on his knees, he withdrew the map from his pocket. Nothing on the paper indicated which of the squiggly lines represented the branch before him or if it was the one rich with pigtoes. Its narrow and rocky appearance convinced him to look for a stream bed with more promise, while a sudden and unexplainable impulse drove him to explore it.

Obie argued with the notion that took him up the steep incline, through a saddle, across the ridge and out onto a layered limestone shelf. Before him, and sweeping over ridges and down valleys, lay a coverlet of variegated reds, yellows and greens, while several hundred feet directly below stretched a flat but irregular-shaped valley. Surprised, then overwhelmed by all that he tried to instantly understand, Obie sank to his knees. "Chaser, will you look at this place. Strange," he whispered.

He had expected to see a heavily forested valley whose bottom housed a mountain creek. Instead, and knowing that nothing in his experience had prepared him for such a contradiction, he saw a wide, dark and slow-moving body of water. Springs and branches, cascading down rocky funnels from the surrounding hollows, fed the riverlike creek, while the remains of tree stumps outlined a broad, rectangular ribbon of cleared ground. At the most southerly end stood a rock fireplace, four walls of a square log cabin bathed in that same foggy blue haze.

Obie backed off, yet an inner and compelling force enticed him, encouraged him to explore the mysterious valley and the untypical flow of water. He blew out his lips as if to relieve himself of some internal pressure. He turned in a circle, thinking he smelled smoke. But he saw no proof of it and studied the lower valley closely to be certain. Spicebush and sassafras were fragrant, too. But he saw no evidence of those either. Finally he raised up. "My common sense tells me we should go back," he said to Chaser, "but I know I'll never be satisfied unless I go down there."

From the shelf of limestone that jutted out over the

valley, Obie came across a narrow trail that took him through a forest overflowing with ferns and lush vegetation, granite rock and bubbling springs, signs of deer and wild boar. At the foot of the trail, he stepped out from the trees and into the open light. Decaying tree stumps, huge and angular shaped graybacks masked by lichens stood like faceless figures in the knee-deep beargrass that reached all the way to the river.

Droplets of morning mist clung to the thin blades and wet the legs of Obie's overalls. As he neared the water and heard the quiet lapping, his pace picked up. "Come on, girl. Maybe this is the right place. It's spooky enough to keep most folk away."

From a short distance off, the creek appeared shallow and he assumed it had a rocky bottom. But the same impulse that brought him over the mountain warned him now against being deceived. He walked upstream. He observed the uncertain depths, breathed in the odors of earth, living green plants, of fish, death and decay.

Rather than stepping off the bank and testing the depth, he found a dead limb and used it as a measuring stick. The limb stood more than twice his height. It struck bottom about one third of its length, and he judged the depth to be nearly four feet . . . at least as far as he could reach.

He dismissed wading out and turned the tow sack upside down. Apples rolled aside. He stretched the rope and grappling line straight. "Chaser, where are—oh," he said. "How come you're not off snooping? This looks like a likely place for squirrel and a dozen or so pearls for me."

He grinned. He found a medium-sized rock and tied it to the line. He felt good about this place now and encouraged by the unexplainable impulse that had brought him over the ridge. That same feeling told him that he would find more pearls than his great-granddaddy Wilks found.

To get the line out as far into the creek as possible, he aimed the rock toward the dark east bank and threw it. It hit. It immediately took the line down. The coil unwound until only a few feet remained. The depth surprised Obie and added to the mysteriousness of the river-like creek. He picked up an apple, wiped it along his shirt sleeve before biting through the tough red blush. Juice dribbled down his chin and he rubbed that away with the sleeve of his flannel shirt. "Chaser," he said, chewing on the apple, "let's see how far we can drag this line."

His dog stayed closer than an arm's length away. Her nostrils flared. She sniffed at the abundance of scents nervously but none sent her scurrying off on an adventurous hunt. Obie reached back and gave her head an affectionate tap. Hazy light warmed her silky-fine coat and filled the cove. Their faint shadows stretched to the river before disappearing into the glassy, gray-green surface. The murky depths kept him from seeing more than a few inches below the brilliant layer while a swirl of rippling water betrayed the hiding places of boulders that waited unseen.

A short distance ahead, Obie gave up dragging the line farther and began to draw it back. Excitement swelled inside his chest. He realized suddenly that he expected to find mussels on the ends of each thin wire. Yet when they emerged from the water into full view, he yelled, "Yowiee! Will you look at the size of these rascals."

He dropped to his knees. Chaser turned her back to the water as if to stand watch over the clearing and encroaching forest. "These are the biggest mussels I've ever seen." Obie withdrew the knife from his pocket and set aside the sheath. The steel flashed against the light before penetrating the seam and sliding into the soft folds of flesh. A gritting, bubbling vibration worked up the blade, through the handle and into his hand. It left him with the same cold, stiff feeling that killing always had. He tried to throw off the sensation along with the upper shell but the sticky brown nacre ran between his fingers like warm blood. Obie's arm quivered. He squeezed his eyes tight shut. When he opened them again, he saw the pearl.

Obie sucked in his breath, cheering his discovery. As he exhaled, his aversion to killing evaporated into the muggy warm air. And he cut into one mussel, then another, thinking now only of pearls and what they meant to his future.

He found six, all larger than the three he found the night before. He tore a piece from the tail of his patched plaid shirt, wrapped the pearls carefully inside, then stuffed the packet down the narrow pocket in the bib of his overalls. He checked the button twice to be positive it was fastened securely. He had no intention of losing what he had just found.

Before Obie finished eating his apple, he cast his line a dozen more times toward the dark and mysterious east bank, adding nineteen pearls to the six in his pocket. He noticed finally that the sun had crossed the center of the sky some time ago, that the shadows now stretching over the clearing were longer and wider, that the muggy air had turned chilly and forecast nightfall. "Chaser," Obie turned quickly and searched his surroundings, "I'd swear I smelled smoke but . . ."

Obie stepped back from the river. He coiled the rope and repacked the tow sack. He would return tomorrow, set off earlier now that he knew the way. No sense in being greedy and having to make his way back in the dark. Besides, Obie recalled Preacher Gibban saying that greediness was a sin against God. "Come on, Chaser, let's get on back and show Bas what we've found." And he snapped his fingers for his dog to follow.

CHAPTER

6

* * *

THE SUN FELL OFF TO THE WEST SOON AFTER OBIE REACHED
the Yuda. He disliked making his way back to the cave
in the dark but disliked the idea of spending the night
alone in the forest even more. He sent Chaser ahead, then
tried to keep up, but the dense undergrowth forced him
to his hands and knees. He bulled his way through the
thicket, kept his head down and used the tow sack to
protect his face from the briars. As darkness covered the
sky and the river pounded inside his head, Obie felt an
urgency to hurry.

He had no rifle, no way of seeing. If a bear, wild boar
or bobcat watered nearby it would likely hear him, pick
up his scent. If its belly was just half as empty as his, the
varmint would jump him faster than a bug jumps stink.
It was too scary thinking of so many *what ifs* and Obie
called for his dog. But the river caught his voice and
carried it downstream.

The Yuda ran faster now; the sound of it deepened. A succession of rapids filled the dark with turbulence, and Obie freed himself from the last thicket. He welcomed the chance to stand, shaking the cramps from his legs before starting down the last rocky and irregular slope.

Smoke . . . ? He smelled it again but this time it carried with it the scent of roasting meat. "Yeah!" Obie yelled, satisfied now that the smoke he smelled earlier obviously came from Bas's fire. "Chaser, come back here."

But she was hungry, too, and had not eaten her fill since leaving home. Home . . . Obie counted the days; over a week now, and he glimpsed splinters of firelight through the trees. He angled away from the river when the bottom flattened, and shouted, "Sure does smell good."

Chaser came partway back, barked, then turned and raced up to the ledge and the roasting meat. "Boy," Obie said, swinging his tow sack into the cave, "I'm hungry enough to eat dry thistle."

"Where the henry you been?" Bas demanded. His voice wore a cold edge. "It's been black as pitch going on an hour."

Obie crouched before the fire. He glanced at Bas curiously and questioned the apparent reason for his anger. But without responding, Obie unbuttoned his pocket and withdrew the packet. "Got something here to show you."

Obie laid back the ends of the flannel torn from his shirt. "Found them in a branch one ridge over."

"That why you couldn't come back before dark? You just got too busy finding pearls."

"What's ailing you?" Obie demanded. "You're carrying on like you got your tongue tangled up in a churn dasher."

Bas refused to respond. Instead of his deliberate and unruffled way, he turned the meat with jerks and starts. The furrows of loose flesh across his forehead deepened while his gaze drove through the flames, the bed of coals, to a hidden region below the shelf of rock.

"Dang it," Obie's voice tingled with irritation, "look at what I found, will you. Twenty-five more to go with the three from last night."

But Bas went on turning the meat, his lips locked tight. "What's the matter with you?" Obie demanded. "You can't be this mad just because I took too long getting back here. And I know that no one from Felker Mountain is afraid of the dark."

The fire blazed between them while the pearls, resting on the cloth, caught the light and gave back an iridescent glow. Yet Bas continued to focus his attention on some thought that took his mind to secret depths. His broad shoulders, hunched forward, gave him the look of a brooding bear. His chin, jaw and cheekbones drew the same sharp lines as the bones jutting out above his blue eyes. "Look," Obie finally said and returned the pearls to his pocket, "I'm sorry. And I really would like to know why you're acting like you butted heads with a tree stump."

Bas lifted the roasting meat from over the fire. He cut generous chunks and threw them to Chaser. Obie started to object; his belly twisted and bucked like a saw going through green oak. But Bas at last raised his eyes and said, "I seen something, seen it late on but I'd been feeling real peculiar the whole day. Part of me was itching to shoot a boar; the other part kept looking back over my shoulder." Bas ran his tongue across his upper lip. "Long toward sundown I headed back to here. About the time I reached crossways with that old cabin, I heared something that sent cold shivers through my heart."

Bas wiped the knife blade on the leg of his overalls. "I heard this awful moan, then this scary, screeching, screaming shriek. I'll tell you true, Obie, I walked a fat circle around that old cabin just as fast as these here legs would carry me." A thin sheen of sweat covered Bas's face. "Weren't until later that I come on the track; biggest bear pads I ever seen."

Bas used his hands to indicate the size. "I ain't lying when I tell you they was near as long as my shoe. Alongside were the track of a man. Fresh, too."

"You saw a shoe print?"

Bas shook his head. "Ain't never seen the track of no Cherokee but Indian's what it looked like; like the print of a moccasin."

Obie's belly rose into his throat. He strained to swallow it back. "You're sure about all of this?"

"I'm a-tellin' you pure gospel. And something else." Bas used the arm of his shirt to wipe the sweat from his forehead. "I smelled smoke the whole day. You build any fires over where you were?"

Obie shook his head. He teetered on the edge of telling Bas that he, too, had smelled smoke.

"Obie," Bas said, "we ain't alone. We's got company."

Obie stared into the fire, then in a low, nasal voice, he said, "But you never saw anyone?"

"Ain't talking about that kinda company." Sweat

62

stuck Bas's blond hair to his forehead. "I'm talking about the booger kind that your daddy met hovering over Claiborne Wilks's burnt-out cabin."

Obie started to laugh; instead, he held his hands out to the fire. His daddy swore to seeing some kind of eerie blue light and hearing a bodiless voice soon after Granddaddy Wilks died in the fire. Of course no one believed him. Everyone said it was just another of his stories. But Obie remembered his daddy setting the Bible on the table, pressing his right hand over the black leather cover and swearing to God that every word was true.

Dalton Wilks drew pleasure from storytelling. His eyes sparkled and a wee-to-nothing sort of smile hid in the lines around his mouth. But when he told about the booger in the burnt-out cabin, not a speck of pleasure showed. And Obie had seen Chaser take a licking rather than go near the ruins.

"Bas," Obie picked up a tin plate and held it out, "if I don't eat real soon there isn't gonna be anything left of me to worry over boogers. Cut me off some of that meat, will you."

Bas's eyes shifted from Obie to the meat, then back to Obie. "You can't eat that."

"Why not?"

"It's cat, that's why. Cat meat ain't fit for a-body to put in his belly."

Obie pushed the plate closer. "It's meat, isn't it?"

"Bobcat ain't meat; only cooked it for Chaser. Dogs won't touch it 'lessen it's cooked."

Obie leaned into the smoke. "Smells fine to me and I want a sizeable portion because I'm as hungry as a landlocked crawdad."

"Your brain's been addled." But Bas drew his knife

63

through the fleshy chunk and offered it to Obie on the end of the blade. His teeth clicked in a long shiver that shook his shoulders and vibrated the length of him as Obie licked the juice from his fingers.

"It's filling," Obie said. "A might sour tasting but filling."

Bas settled back on his heels and watched Obie chew. Each time he swallowed, Bas scrunched up his face as if he had a terrible bellyache. Obie ate five slices before he helped himself to the kettle of mush. He poured molasses over a generous amount and ate the last of the bacon. "For a little feller," Bas said, "you got a horse-sized appetite. If you take to meowing and jumping round on your tippy-toes I'll knowd it was that cat you ate."

Obie grinned. "Aren't you gonna ask me about the pearls? I found them all in one short stretch of stream bed."

"I ain't forgotten what you found but it's them noises I heared, the smoke I smelled and them prints. That's what's prodding my mind."

Obie nodded yet he pointed toward the south. "I trailed the Yuda like I told you I was aiming to do, then took off southeast when I came on a branch. I took a path over a low ridge to a valley. There's an old cabin there with a caved-in roof and some bottom that was once cleared; the rest is wooded."

Obie considered telling Bas about the mountain creek that looked almost like a deep and slow-moving river, about the fuzzy blue haze that hung above the cabin, about the illusive scent of smoke. But those things contradicted nature and Obie reached inside his pocket. "You want to carry your half of the pearls?"

"No need." Bas threw Chaser a meaty bone. "How far you say it was to that place you found them pearls?"

"Over that next ridge."

"And you didn't smell no smoke?" Bas asked, his face full of concern.

Obie disliked lying but it seemed a sensible thing to do and shook his head. "But I did see sign of deer and wild boar. I'm going back over there tomorrow and you're welcome to come along. You can hunt while I'm pearling."

With squinted eyes and lips drawn tight against his teeth, Bas shook his head. "I ain't budging from this here cave, and I think we outta give serious thought to going home." Bas poked another piece of wood into the fire. "I ain't good with numbers but if that wee-bitty pearl Micager Wilks found is worth the fifty dollars you say, then them you got there ought to be worth more. Figure for me, Obie, fifty times twenty-eight. That's how many you got, ain't it?"

Obie crawled into the cave for his quilt. He rolled up in it before sitting cross-legged on his pallet. "It comes to fourteen hundred."

"Dollars?" Bas eyes stood round as saucers. "Feller with that much money can park hisself out front of Amos Dryer's General Store and not do a lick of work his whole life. It's time we was going home, Obie."

Obie turned his back to the fire. He stared at the dark night, listened to the river. He had lied to Bas about his great-granddaddy's pearl being worth fifty dollars. Obie untied his left shoe. He loosened the laces, pulled back the tongue, then slid it from his foot. He untied the second high-top shoe and placed it alongside the other before stretching flat on his pallet.

Obie disliked his brother Virg because he lied. He disliked Virg because he could never be counted on. Now Obie had lied to Bas but made excuses for his lies and gave those excuses importance. That little pearl of Micager Wilks's was worth no more than a few dollars. Obie stared at the fire. Twenty years ago, the pearls in his pocket would have brought three times what he expected to get now. *Dang Depression!* Now, and if he was lucky, they might bring three hundred dollars; his half would not begin to settle his daddy's debt to Mr. Arvis Cagley.

"Obie, we kin light outta here come sunup."

Obie closed his eyes. He could not think about going home until he had at least twice twenty-eight.

"Obie, you asleep?"

Obie squeezed his eyes tight shut. He closed out the sound of the river and all the night noises, but the guilt within him refused to be shut away and prodded him to amend his lies. Obie turned his back and drifted off into a deep, troubled sleep.

His head whirled like a top until his neck twisted and caused his body to turn, too. He spun in a tiny, slow circle. As the turning continued the circle grew elliptical and Obie felt himself being hurtled ahead. He passed Virg, who laughed like a braying jackass, passed Bas, shaking an accusing finger. But when the spinning stopped and Obie fell to earth, he dropped at the feet of an old man . . . caved in cheeks, hollow eye sockets, thin lips, wrinkled brown face. Was he a Cherokee? A Nun Yuna Wi? An Immortal? Obie had no way of knowing.

The old man wore doeskins; a tangle of moss and vines

66

covered his coarse black hair. His skin was rough like a fence lizard's. He caught hold of Obie. Then with long, bony fingers, he drew Obie up and set him on his bare feet.

Was this old man the legendary stone man?

Obie squeezed his eyes tight. He opened them; the old man continued to stare. Obie sucked in his cheeks. He felt the need to speak, to explain without knowing what needed explaining. He smiled until he saw the crooked stick in the old man's hand. The stick looked more like rock than wood. When he raised it above his head, his black eyes showed splinters of orange and purple.

He slashed the crooked white stick across the sky but drew back a glistening knife blade. He swung it the length of Obie's body. A pain shot through Obie's belly, between his ribs, and he cried out, "Who are you? What is it you want?"

The responding voice made no sound, yet Obie saw the lips move and he understood: the pearls belonged to the river, to the spirit who planted the seed inside the mussel. They were not Obie's to harvest.

The old man pointed the glistening knife tip at Obie's heart. "Wait," Obie cried out, then explained why he needed the pearls, ". . . for taxes and my daddy's debt to Mr. Arvis Cagley."

The old man threw back his head. He turned his face to the sky. He called out with strange words and in a language unknown to Obie. Wind rose from the calm with such force that it silenced the river. It bent ancient chestnuts to the ground, ripped hemlocks apart. Slivered splinters burst through the vaporous blue haze like needles. Thunder shook the earth; it swirled the river into a turbulent frenzy. A convulsion of waves somersaulted over the bank. Water smothered the belly deep beargrass and left it writhing in the *fat black bottom. Lightning exploded. Its track raced across the black day and slithered over the horizon. But it was the wind and its brutal force that tore Obie's hair from his head, that hurtled him into the air, then threw him back and entangled him in a lariat of sorrel vine.*

Obie screamed. *"God, help me. Please, God."*

"Obie!" Bas pulled him up by the bib of his overalls. "Wake up, Obie. I told you that cat weren't fit to put in your belly. Obie, open your eyes."

Obie stared at the orange coals, the dark enclosing them. He blinked, then blinked again. He shook his head, tried to refocus his thoughts. But the dream hovered like a ghost and refused to relinquish his mind.

"Obie? Obie, you hear me talking to you?" Bas's persistence broke through the barrier. "What the devil ails you?"

"I hear you." Obie attempted to swallow the dream in one gulp but it refused to be forgotten. The most vivid details pressed upon him. "I had a dream."

"Sounded more like you had a scarebooger after you."

Obie looked over Bas's shoulder and into the cave—a hollow black hole. A stick, crooked and white, danced in circles. Obie hurriedly turned away. "I was dreaming that a wind storm caught me, that's all."

He ran his hand over his head and squeezed his hair between his fingers. It had been a dream and the dancing stick inside the cave was part of the same dream. But when Obie pressed that place between his ribs, he flinched. Tears filled his eyes.

"What's ailing you? You get yourself hurt or something?"

68

Obie shook his head. "Must have been lying on a rock. I'm okay."

Obie stretched the length of his pallet. He pressed against Chaser when she came and dropped beside him. He stared at the coals. The terror he felt was real. Could the dream have been something more than a dream? A prophecy, maybe?

CHAPTER

7

* * *

OBIE AWOKE TO A BLAZING FIRE, A DAMP, OVERCAST MORNing, the smell of boiled coffee and frying bacon. Bas
watched him from across the fire while Chaser's tail
thumped his leg. "Morning," Obie said, and sat up cross-
legged.

"You're smelling the last of the bacon." Bas filled
both tin cups with coffee. "And there ain't a whole lot of
this left neither. I'm for going home." Bas sucked up the
hot coffee. "Heard frogs a-croaking last night. Weather
kin turn plumb fierce in no time."

Obie left the cup set on the ground. "Could it be
that you're wanting to go home has more to do with
what happened yesterday than the weather? You were
scared."

"Durn right I were skeered and I ain't ashamed to
admit it neither. I got me a healthy respect for things I
can't explain," he said. "'Sides that, it's gonna take us a

mite longer to find our way outta these hills than it did coming. There's that river to cross; you got them two quarters, ain't you?"

Obie nodded before reaching deep in his pocket to feel them beside Micager's map.

"Good thing," Bas said. "I can't see no sense in staying longer since you got what you come for."

"But I haven't." Obie slid his foot into the left shoe first. He concentrated on pushing each lace through the proper eye rather than facing Bas. "I lied to you about Micager Wilks's pearl being worth fifty dollars. It's not."

Obie drew the laces snug. He tied them. Rather than releasing the bow, he continued to hold on, to pull the knot even tighter. To let go would call for an immediate explanation. It would force him to look up, to confront the criticism that fired the coals between them. Obie reached for the second shoe but his arms stiffened before he slipped his foot inside. "The pearls, here inside my pocket . . ." Obie paused. Pearls were bringing near twenty dollars each according to Mr. Aaron Smith in Nashville. But Obie said, "These pearls, here inside my pocket, might bring ten dollars each; twenty if we're lucky. So far—" Obie's voice faltered "—half won't even pay off my daddy's debt. I can't go home."

Bas sat silent for a long while before he asked, "How come you lied? There was no need; you knowd it weren't the money that brung me."

Obie stared at the shoe, at the dark inside. Why? An answer escaped him . . . being the oldest . . . dammit! He had looked for work, would have taken anything to earn money.

"Once," Bas said, "I heard you yell at Virg for lying.

You called him a no-account. That what you are, a no-account liar?"

The pressure to be understood welled within Obie until he jammed his foot into the right shoe and blurted, "I lied because I had no other choice. I was afraid to come here alone."

Obie hugged his knees. It had been necessary to lie. He had done it with such confidence; the lie would provide what his family needed. "When I realized that the only hope I had for saving Wilks Hollow was to find pearls, I made up the lie about the value of Micager's pearl. I figured that would persuade Virg to come with me. He's greedy as a buzzard and a Wilks, too. But Virg laughed at my idea to save the farm. He laughed!"

Obie kicked at a loose rock. "Before I could decide what to do, you showed up and asked to come along. It never seemed important to tell you the truth. It was easier to let it pass."

"But the other night—"

"I know," Obie interrupted. "I know I told you it was worth fifty dollars. I told you that because I knew you were scared. I thought I had to convince you to stay."

"It weren't the money that brung me. How many times I got to tell you that?"

"But it brought me!" Obie snapped back. "I had to do something; I couldn't let you light out for home and leave me here alone. I don't own a rifle; I couldn't hit a jackass turned broadsides if I had to. I brought along every bit of food my mamma could spare. Now there's less than a little bit left. I need you to stay, to hunt for our food."

Bas stretched his legs straight. His shoes, as they slid

over the rock, made a sharp, scraping noise. "What about that pearl in Traskville being worth a thousand dollars? That another lie?"

No! Before the Depression it would have brought that much. But Obie shook his head, refusing now to make another excuse. He had given the pearl an exaggerated value to impress Bas in hopes that would persuade him to stay.

"Well," Bas said with thoughtfully puckered lips, "it don't matter no never mind. You take my half of the pearls. That'll give you plenty."

Three hundred dollars would pay the debt, taxes owed and something extra for his mamma. But there would be nothing left for his plans. Again Obie shook his head. "I promised shares, Bas, promised them long before we left home and I'm not one to go back on my word once I give it."

"I told you I don't give diddly-squat about sitting in the catbird seat. I just want to get on home."

"But I can't!"

"Whatcha mean you can't ?"

"I have to do the right thing. Us Wilkses got a reputation for being honorable."

"You all got reputations for being stubborn as Collin's ram." Bas drove a spoon into the kettle of mush and plopped a mound on the tin plate. He held the bacon between his fingers, chewed while he said, "I ain't going back home without you. Ain't gonna be me that tells your mamma I left you behind. Ain't gonna give that woman no cause to low-rate us Allardices anymore."

"She doesn't know that you're with me."

"But Virg do and he'd sure as henry tell her, too."

While Obie ate his half of the bacon and plate of mush, he kept one eye turned on Bas. The moonshiner's boy was no more like Virg Wilks than a garden snake resembled a copperhead. Obie liked Bas, wished they could be friends, but his mamma would never allow it. She swore before God and everyone that she'd shoot any Allardice fool enough to set foot on Wilks's land. And his mamma had a long-lasting unforgiving streak.

Bas wiped his shirt sleeve across his mouth. "You want me to come up to that valley with you?"

"Thought you said you weren't budging from this spot?"

"I did. And if I'm to get my pickings, I'll keep Chaser and stay right here the whole blessed day."

Obie reached for Chaser and started to object. He wanted to say, "No, I want her along with me." "Sure," Obie replied, "she'll probably like staying here. Maybe she can scare up some squirrel for supper if you should decide to do some hunting. But I'll eat more of that bobcat if that's all there is."

Bas drew his nose and mouth to one side in a terrible stink. "If you don't get back, like last evening, I ain't coming to look for you."

"If I'm not back before dark, I'd be grateful if you'd set a fire to burning. That'll help me find my way. Bas . . ." Obie hesitated like someone searching for something buried very deep. "Thank you for not knocking me silly. Virg would have pounded me bloody."

"You and your brother carry a heavy load of cussedness for each other."

It was true, though Obie had no idea where it came from or how it started. He remembered it from the summer Virg grew six inches and stopped listening to reason.

Finally Obie gathered up his tow sack and set off. He walked with a bounce, whistled some and felt lighter now that the lies were from his shoulders. A few hours later, he followed the Yuda, then turned south at the trail. He moved through the thinning haze and up the ridge. He stopped when reaching the saddle. From the limestone ledge, above the valley, he searched the sky for a sign that might bear out Bas's suspicions.

Obie knew the old superstitions about bats flying in daytime and frogs croaking all night; he had heard such talk his whole life . . . storytelling, old wives tales. But nothing he saw, in any direction, confirmed Bas's belief that a weather change was inevitable.

The sun hung over the mountains like a brilliant circle of tin foil, fuzzied by a vaporous gray veil. The damp haze would burn off; the day might even turn hot. Beneath it all, the valley rested as quietly as Graysonia Cemetery.

Obie threw open his coat. He missed Chaser not being along; she added to his courage. He took a deep breath of air, then gave it back. Admitting to being scared never seemed to bother Bas. Obie wondered why it bothered him, why it left him angry and out of sorts.

Obie hoisted the tow sack over his shoulder. He found his way to the game trail that took him down. Patches of pale sunlight fell through autumn-colored trees and worked across Obie's face. He skip-walked a short distance before layers of dry leaves caused him to trip forward. He slowed to a walk. Risking a turned ankle was dumb, especially now, when he counted on finding more pearls than yesterday. Maybe as many as forty.

Such a possibility caused him to laugh. It felt good to laugh. He laughed louder and longer. Laughing lessened the uneasiness of not having Chaser along. Obie sucked in cool, musty air as he weaved around the thickets. He spent more than a moment wondering if this was the exact place Micager Wilks found his pearls and saw the Nun Yuna Wi. There was no way to be certain. Too many branches and spring branches, too many creeks that drained down from the heavily forested hollows into the Yuda. Obie hoped that Micager Wilks found his pearl in another valley. Off in another direction, miles from where he now stood, where the Nun Yuna Wi were watching over the giant pigtoe and cave of pearls.

When Obie reached the flat and started across, his pant legs picked up the dew still clinging to the grass while the warmth reached through his coat and shirt. Rather than returning to the spot he worked the day before, he moved farther south. He carried within him an expectant excitement, which added a spring to his step.

The river made an easy bend and Obie settled in the arc of it. Before he dumped his tow sack, he took a long and careful look around. Off to the south for a hundred yards at least stood open ground, a broad line of old stumps, then forest. Behind him and to the north was the same. Across the river, a sheer rock face stretched up to a high ledge and reached out long arms in both directions. Satisfied, Obie emptied the tow sack: grappling line, thin wire, knife, hatchet, sharpening stone and raw turnips.

Obie pried a rock from the riverbank and attached it to the grappling line, threw it toward the center with great confidence, then watched it hit shy and take the line to the bottom. He towed it slowly upstream before pulling it in. Three ripplebacks clung to the wires but none held a pearl in its soft mantle. Obie lightened the weight on the line and aimed it farther. Again, he pulled the line south before drawing it in. A collection of small and empty mussels clung to the wires. He discarded the shells by throwing them as far across the river as his strength allowed. He wished for muscles the size of his brother's. Wasn't right, him being the oldest and so small. He had a craw full of Virg laughing and strutting like a rooster. Obie slung the line as far as he could. Watched it settle in the deep center trough before he moved upstream. It seemed only right that being the oldest should mean being the biggest and strongest. Every Sunday and once during the week, he sat in Graysonia's biggest church and prayed. He asked God why He saw fit to make him so short and puny. Since God never sent him a growing streak, he assumed that God just needed another feist.

Obie faced the murky, slow-moving water and drew the line back, empty. "Dang it!" Had he found the river's only mussel bed yesterday? He slammed the line to the ground. He kicked at it and whirled in a full circle. He raised his damp face to the sky. "How come," he yelled, "how come, when a fellow tries to do the right thing, You don't help out? How come?"

Obie drove both fists deep in his pockets. His vision of the river blurred and for no reason, he remembered something his mamma said, *"If it's worth doing, Obadiah, it's worth doing right, even if right means doing it over and over and over."*

Obie respected his mamma's wisdom but it seemed, this being a family problem, that Virg owned a share of the responsibility. Seemed unfair that all of it should fall on his shoulders.

Obie gathered his belongings and marched upstream. He stopped before the river turned into a brawling, rock-strewn series of rapids. A short distance to the right, shadows reached out as if to shake hands. Rather than welcomed, Obie felt uncomfortable, plagued suddenly by an eerie sense of an illusive presence hovering about him. Several times he turned in a slow, complete circle. Why did he feel as if he walked in the footsteps of his great-granddaddy, of Cherokees who lived and died in this valley? What caused him to feel this presence of someone else? Surely the sensation came from more than his imagination. Obie studied the line of trees; his mind took him deeper into the dense and untamed world of shadows and indistinguishable sounds. Again, was it imagination or were those sounds that he continued to hear the sounds of moccasined feet and the whispers of old voices? Was he being influenced by Bas's fears and his own dreams?

Obie threw the grappling line into the river. He let it settle and rest upon the bottom while he collected rock from that stretch of river that turned into a brawling series of rapids. He hollowed a place near the river where the ground was moist and easy to dig, then lined it with rock. Next, he gathered firewood from the edge of the forest and lit a fire inside the pit. When he finally drew in the line, he saw that each thin wire held at least one mussel, sometimes two and three.

Obie cleared the line before throwing it back. He sat cross-legged on the grassy bank and began opening mussels. He threw the top half into a pile, probed the mantle for a pearl, then placed the meaty half close to the fire to cook in its own shell. Gritty mussels added something to his near-empty belly besides raw turnips. When he had finished opening the mussels, two more pearls were added to his collection of twenty-eight.

While the mussels cooked, Obie drew the line upstream before bringing it in. Each time that he performed the maneuver, he added at least one more pearl to the growing number. Yet he sensed that the river continually made promises and each promise drew him deeper into the valley and its dark depths.

He no longer saw the fire or his tow sack as he followed the wide bend to the rapids, climbed the loose rock and gravel incline to a new height of quiet and deep running water. Forest pushed to the creek's edge on both sides and left Obie uncertain.

He threw the line out, watched it hit and send forth a wake of spiraling ripples. As the water settled, a golden leaf floated past. It turned slowly on top of the current. Like a whisper, he thought, a whisper carried along by the unseen current.

Was the river the cause of his uneasiness? What were its promises luring him toward? Did it have secrets hidden beneath its greenness? Something sudden and swift, off to the side, blurred across the corner of his vision. Leaves rustled behind him. He stiffened. He turned his head slowly and aimed his ear at the sound. It stopped. Branches whipped the warm, still air, then the rustling began again. It moved closer. A twig snapped. Alarm crept along Obie's spine. His heart shot into his throat. His only escape was the river. He would swim for the other side if it was Bas's mysterious moccasined spirit. Obie whirled around, intent upon confronting his silent assailant.

A white-tailed deer jerked its head erect, bolted upright, then whirled on its hind legs and sprang for the forest's safety. Obie stared at the dark green tunnel through which the deer escaped.

Grateful there were no witnesses to his stupidity, Obie backed to the water. He chided himself further and criticized the fear that made every sound a threat. He even laughed at his dreams and Bas's mysterious spirit; yet an unspoken foreboding inside his throat stifled the amusement. Angry with himself, he spun around and jerked up the line. When gray, nubbly and irregular shaped mussels broke the surface a new wave of expectancy pushed all other thoughts aside.

He cut into them hurriedly. A pearl, larger than a pea, worth a hundred at least. But he knew, too, that the price of pearls depended upon the man doing the buying. Obie added three more to the growing packet. He counted thirty-six, smiled while realizing that all of the afternoon waited.

He rewound the rope and walked farther upstream. Shadows and rustling leaves, like his dreams, followed close behind. He ignored the dreams, the threat of being swallowed up, the restless sounds that kept after him from inside the forest. He caught himself holding his breath and turning his head to listen. But the sounds were as elusive as birds flitting from tree to tree. Finally he decided upon a likely spot and returned the line to the water.

The sun's warmth and the feel of it across his neck made light of Bas's forecast. Green spruce and gray rock stood crisp against the blue sky while a V of geese passed to the south. Obie loved autumn. At home it meant butchering hogs and smoking meat, his mamma making hominy and apple butter, canning pumpkin for winter pies, and he felt his stomach pinch. It meant cutting down trees, chopping wood, stacking it. It meant snugging up and settling in, time for reading, storytelling, making popcorn and helping Orrie cut paper dolls. But his fond reminiscing ended abruptly.

A shadow dropped across the water. It disappeared almost as quickly as it appeared. He swung around. A chill raced the length of his body and raced back up. He waited and watched. He dared it to reappear with short, uneven breaths.

Hightail it! But he shook off the notion, decided that it had been a buzzard passing overhead. Obie took several deep breaths before redirecting his attention to the line.

Minutes passed into hours as he continued the mechanics of throwing the line out, then pulling it in, removing the mussels and finding an occasional pearl. Yet his mind remained alert to the sounds at his back.

He felt watched, as if someone waited just out of sight. Was his imagination responding to his fears, to last night's dream? Were those fears justified? At home he laughed about boogers, gave no stock to dreams, and the Nun Yuna Wi were fanciful nonsense. But here in River Country, he thought, it all became real. And that entrapped him.

An agony of fright twisted his thoughts further and filled his mouth with an ugly taste. He had smelled the same smoke Bas had smelled, smelled it several times. Obie faced the thick wall of trees. He considered exploring beyond the fringe but never without Chaser. Could a fellow have wide-awake dreams the same as the sleeping kind? He sucked in his cheeks while his heart threatened to wear itself out, beating hard.

Obie shook his head and returned to the creek. The rope he had left on the bank floated downstream. He started after it but the creek and its dark center trough wore a menacing mask that made him hesitate. Without the rope . . .

Obie threw off his coat and shoes. He jumped in, stretched out and began to swim. He made perfect strokes but before the rope was within reach, the current caught him. It drew him toward the center trough. Along the bottom, Obie felt a second pull on his legs. It turned. It twisted. It started him moving in a slow circular motion. *Sucking pot!*

He chopped through the surface, drew back with every bit of his strength and kicked. It would do no good to save himself and lose the rope. He reached out farther, pulled back faster. He swam with both eyes open. Besides catching hold of the rope, he knew the rapids lay ahead, maybe a sucking pot, too. He knew if he took too much time in reaching the rope, he would never free himself from the current that continued to control him.

Obie arched his back. He dove beneath the surface, looked for a submerged rock that might provide him with enough leverage to spring ahead, grab the rope and haul himself out before being dragged into the chute and shot over the rapids. He might survive. Then again . . .

Ahead, a row of huge boulders stretched across the stream bed. Beyond them . . . Obie flailed at the water, kicked until he caught hold of the rope, then angled toward that corner between the bank and first large boulder that would stop him from being swept down the rapids. But the current and the heaviness of the rock-weighted line carried him toward the chute. He refused to let loose. Without the rope there would be no more pearls. He extended his arms, pulled back until they ached. The sockets stung. "Damn you, Virg Wilks! Why ain't you here to help out?"

Obie's lungs filled with murky green water; it blurred his vision but the approaching danger wrung from him a last burst of energy. His feet hit submerged rocks. He sprang ahead until he finally dug his toes into the soft bottom. He pushed toward the bank, lunged when the beargrass was within reach.

He lay there, his body a spasm of pain, his lungs threatening to explode, but it was the thought of the pearls in his pocket that brought him to his knees. He grabbed at the pocket with both hands. His fingers clutched the bulge and extinguished the fear. "Lord," he whispered, "You were sure watching out for me this time." But when he looked back at the creek, he shouted, "You near drowned me, you dang creek!"

Obie worked the line onto the bank. He counted twenty some mussels on the wires. He should have been excited yet he eyed them suspiciously. He knew there were pearls inside the ripplebacks, knew that there would be more than all the other times, knew that the pearls would be bigger, too. He looked off to the south. Something hid out there; whatever or whoever, it was partners with the river and he was being tempted, just like Jesus had been tempted.

Obie took his time opening the mussels and added another three pearls to the packet. He decided to head back even though an hour of daylight remained, when he remembered his coat and shoes. His mamma would have a conniption if he left them behind. And Obie knew how her conniptions could stretch into week-long periods of silence, side-glances and sneers.

Fear of his mamma's ire outweighed his fear of the forest and he raced back, refusing to look in any direction except ahead. He found them, tucked them under his arm and whirled about. Hurriedly but carefully he picked his way down the steep incline that paralleled the rapids, then broke into a run, returning to that place where he had left the mussels cooking.

The coals retained specks of color. But the mussels were gone. A bear? 'Possum, maybe? Would they eat shells and all? Obie bit his lip . . . *not likely*. He stuffed his curiosity into the tow sack with his other belongings and cut across the clearing. Near the center, a moaning sort of scream filled the air, a sound like his mamma made when giving birth to Loranda.

He ran faster until reaching the shadows of the forest. A wave of black bats forced him to duck, while the blazing sunset was made stagnant by gray-green clouds. Was Bas right? Was a storm on its way?

Besides finding the pearls, he had to get them home. There was the Sallapoosa to cross, then the big river. Obie jammed his hand into his pocket, past Micager's soggy map to the . . . the quarters? They were gone! Without them . . . the big river was too wide for swimming and November first was too close for going by way of Scagg's Ford.

"Damn you!" Obie shouted and swung back to glare at the creek. He raised a fist but before he shook it, a low, trailing moan rushed at him from the valley floor. Its fleeting breath touched his cheek, his wet clothes and sent a shiver his length.

Obie ran now, ran without thought of his footing or the dangers that might lurk behind every dark thicket. When he reached the ledge, he paused only long enough to catch his breath and glance back. An eerie gold light washed over the valley while a colony of shadows peopled the bottom. Obie rushed down the other side with just one thought: If he ever got free of Micager Wilks's River Country he would never return.

CHAPTER

8

* * *

THEY STOOD ON OPPOSITE SIDES OF THE FIRE WHILE OBIE turned his pockets inside out. "I must have lost them when I jumped in to save the line." But his fingers continued to pull on the empty pockets as if that might produce the missing coins.

"If that Mr. Torrey won't swap us a trip across the river in his boat for a pearl, we got ourselves a longsum walk."

"With no chance for a ride and time we don't have." Obie removed his wet clothes and arranged them before the fire while calculating the miles home and the remaining days before the first of the month. He wedged his teeth together to stop their trembling, then added, "I'm dang near froze."

"Wrap up in this here quilt and drink that coffee I give you. It ain't strong enough to curl baby hair but it's soothing to the belly."

Bas stirred the soot-blackened kettle. "Can't believe you only found three pearls. I figured sure you'd get a dozen."

Obie stared into the fire. He felt guilty lying to Bas again. But if he told him the truth, that they now had forty-one pearls instead of thirty-one, Bas would insist they head off for home. Obie sipped the coffee because it was too hot to drink. If Bas could only understand how important going north was to him, then he wouldn't have to lie or invent reasons for delaying the trip home. But with the loss of the quarters, could he delay it any longer? Did he dare take such a gamble? His gaze shifted slowly until he looked into Bas's broad face. "I can't believe that all you got for our supper are two puny squirrel."

Bas leaned toward the kettle to smell the aroma rising off the stew. "Chaser and me set here a spell after you lit out. But it weren't no fun. So me and her went hunting."

Bas gave the dog's ear a playful tug. "Besides them two squirrel you smell stewing, the only other thing I saw were one rabbit. Sure as a dead man stinks, Obie, that there rabbit were the sorriest looking critter I ever laid my eye to. Skinny, scrawny, scraggly necked thing what wouldn't make a fit broth. So I said to Chaser here, that poor little feller is so near dead that shooting him would be a plumb waste."

Obie studied Bas's tightly drawn lips, then laughed. "That's about the sorriest story I ever heard you tell."

"Ain't no story; it's gospel."

"Sure it is." Obie tightened the quilt around his shoulders. "I'm telling you, Bas, my belly is as empty as a vacant house. Sure would like some of my mamma's stewed potatoes, fried okra, egg custard, blackberry dumplings, ham and shuck-beans with hot biscuits and red-eye gravy."

Bas let out a pitiful cry and hugged his middle. "We best stop all this make-believe and get to eating what we got, which ain't much."

Bas spooned equal portions of the squirrel and shuck-bean stew onto tin plates. "I cooked Chaser the rest of that cat. Ain't nothing wrong with her rations. Lookie there at her fat belly."

Chaser lay on her side, her brown eyes closed, the tip of her tail moving slightly. Obie smiled, grateful that he didn't have to share his supper. "Tomorrow," he said, "I could use your help. There's a wide, quiet stretch on the Yuda—"

"Yuda?" Bas wiped his mouth along the sleeve of his shirt. "Tomorrow we're carrying ourselves out of this here place."

Obie licked his fingers. "Can't go, Bas. Not yet."

"Can't go! Obie, we got hardly no food left; weather's sure to turn sour and you got a pocketful of them pearls."

"We got fifteen each."

"You got thirty-one. That's three hundred dollars and then some." Bas leaned closer. "I'm telling you, Obie, we got to be on our way out of this here place."

Obie spooned up the last bit of broth from his plate. "It's like you said, Bas, we'll have to pay that Mr. Torrey with pearls. If he's a greedy man—"

"Greedy? 'Pears to me that you're being the greedy one."

Flames blazed up from the fire. *"He that is greedy of*

gain troubleth his own house" was what his mamma said to Mr. Arvis Cagley when he came up Wilks Hollow looking for payment on the note. Obie poked at the coals with a stick before throwing it into the flames. He wasn't being greedy. Besides the debt and taxes, a little something extra for his mamma, Obie wanted a few dollars in his pocket for the trip north. "This thing I need you to help me build is called a scow."

"You deaf?" Bas asked. "We're going home. If you don't get that money to Mr. Arvis Cagley when that paper says it's due, you Wilkses is sure to be fighting fire with a short broom. You thought on that?"

"We'll make it on time," Obie answered. "I can't leave this place until I have at least sixty pearls."

"Sixty? You fall down and addle your brains?" Bas's tongue came out and flicked across his upper lip. "'Pears to me, Obadiah Wilks, that greed's took hold of your common sense."

"I'm not greedy," Obie lashed back. "I got plans."

"Plans? What sorta plans?" When Obie refused to respond, Bas said, "'Lessen you tell me what's inside your head, we're going home. I'll tote you if I have to."

Obie stared into the dark eyes across the fire for a long while before he said, "Soon as I settle up my daddy's debts, I'm heading north."

"Nawth?" Bas shook his head in disbelief. "Why you want to do that? Ain't nothing up there 'cepting unfriendly folk all scrunched on top of one another and peeing in the same pot. How come you want to go there?"

He recognized Bas's squinted stare, studied it until he felt obliged to say, "I'm going north to make something of myself, just like my uncle Tully done. You remember him, don't you?"

"I remember." Bas sucked on his teeth while a puzzled stare froze his features. "What's wrong with how you is? You got more learning than most folk. You talk proper. You don't use your fingers for counting. Folks like you fine. My daddy says you're the only responsible Wilks, even more so than your daddy were."

Obie loosened his grip on the quilt and let it fall open at the throat. The sudden compliment left him warm and he said, "I can't build the scow and get it in the river without your help."

Bas picked up a rock, rolled it between his thumb and forefinger before he said, "If I stay to help you, I want your word that we'll turn for home day after tomorrow."

"You have my word," Obie promised, then quickly fell into telling Bas about pictures of flat-bottomed barges. "Pearl companies use scows to drag the big rivers. The contraption that's pulled behind the barge is called a crow's foot. It's a simple sort of drag, has a wood frame and long chains that hang down. At the end of each chain there's a four-pronged grapple."

"You telling me that we're gonna build a flat-bottomed barge in one day? Obie, I knowd your brains has sprung a leak."

"Wait until I finish telling you," Obie shot back. "It's not near as hard as it sounds."

And Obie began: "We'll cut down a few sapling trees, lash them together with whatever vine we can find. Once we get it in the river, I'll ride it downstream to a sand bar I saw. The drag will follow behind, raking through a deep trough. Bas," Obie caught his breath, "that stretch of the Yuda is gentle as a newborn. And there's pearls in there. I know it."

Bas's doubts drew deep lines around his mouth. "You know, don't you, there's sucking pots in these here rivers. Just how you aim to guide such a thing if you get caught in one of them swirls?"

"I still have to figure that out," Obie admitted. "My daddy used to say that sleeping on a notion was sure to hatch up an answer."

"Your daddy was a sure-enough tower of Babel."

Obie grinned. "He did like to talk, all right."

"Probably talk hisself right out of hell, too." Bas rolled up from the fire, shook the kinks from his long legs. "If I ever get this here body home again, ain't nobody gonna get me off Felker Mountain." Bas scoured the kettle clean. After he returned with a pot of fresh water, he stretched the length of his pallet. "When you go nawth, whatcha aim to do?"

"Gonna work with my uncle Tully. He said he'd get me on making automobiles anytime I wanted. He's real high up."

"You told your mamma that you're a-going?"

"Told no one except you."

"Your mamma is sure to throw a screaming fit when she learns of it," Bas said. "Never met a more terrible tempered woman than your mamma."

Obie drew the quilt tight against the chill working its way across his shoulders. He knew about his mamma's fits of poor disposition. Wasn't that she threw things or swore like some womenfolk, but his mamma had a spiteful, mean streak and a way of turning her silence into a weapon. "Last time Uncle Tully was to home—"

"How many times he been home? I only seen him that once."

"That was the only time . . . four years ago. He came up the hollow on a Sunday morning, driving his fancy blue roadster. He brought gardenia perfume for Mamma, tobacco for Daddy and jellied orange slices for us young-guns. He drove me and my sisters to church. Never seen a wad of money like the one he pulled from his pocket when they passed the collecting plate." Obie shook his head. "He was something to behold . . . all dressed up in a white suit and wearing shoes to match. Don't think I'll ever forget how seeing him made me feel. That's when I decided that I was gonna go north and make something of myself like my uncle Tully done."

Bas pulled a pine needle from his pallet and slipped it between his teeth. "Ain't they got hard times up nawth, same as down here?"

"My uncle Tully ain't poor folk. He's real high up, told my daddy that he had a whole passel of men working under him."

"My granny always preached to us boys that a man's worth was to be measured by what he done, not by how he earned his money." Bas raised to an elbow. "You're welcome to my quilt for the night."

"Thanks." Obie considered Bas's comment, then turned his back to the fire.

The warmth reached out and robbed the chilly breeze of its bite. But with the wind came the sound of his mamma's foot tapping the scrubbed pine floor as she rocked back and forth, her eyes half closed, her lips repeating her mind's prayer. Obie recalled the countless troubled times and his mamma saying, "*I may have my* back against the wall but I ain't whupped yet. I'll find us a way outta this here fix. You'll see."

He knew she'd not take lightly his decision to go north. She'd go stone still like she did the day his daddy talked on building a still. His daddy wore the pants in the Wilks family all right, but his mamma was the suspenders that held up them pants. Obie remembered his daddy saying, "I've slept next to that woman near twenty year but there ain't a week goes by that she don't show me another side. Just ain't no figuring her out. Waste of a man's time trying." And his daddy would walk off mumbling to himself, mumbling about Mattie Mae Wilks being the contrariest woman that ever escaped hell. "Ain't a man living ever gonna understand her. No sirree, that woman's a puzzle . . . got more pieces hidden than what's showing on the table."

Obie agreed; there was no sure way of knowing how riled his mamma would get over his going north, no sure way of knowing the steps she would take to stop him. But he knew she would try.

Before Obie settled in, he rebuilt the fire. Come morning he wanted his clothes to be dry. But when Obie threw off the quilts some hours later and slipped into his overalls, their dampness made him shiver. He buttoned the flannel shirt to the throat, pulled on stiff socks and shoes before waking Bas.

Obie boiled the last of the coffee and cooked a pot of mush. He divided it evenly and covered both helpings with plenty of molasses. It tasted sweet and hot, soothing as it went down. After eating his fill, Obie called to Chaser. She stretched up from the ground, yawned and strolled over to Obie's side to lick his plate clean. "You're the best dog there is," he said, and gave her an affectionate hug.

"If you're ready," Obie added, and dragged his tow sack from inside the cave. He raised it over his shoulder. "The walk's a short piece but there are laurel slicks and blackberry hells. Poison ivy, too!"

Sunlight brightened the eastern sky as they left the cave behind. They followed close beside the rocky and turbulent rapids to avoid the dense undergrowth. As the slope gentled and the hollow widened, the vegetation pushed out to the edge of the river and forced them to their hands and knees when the thicket became nearly impassable.

Obie led the way; Chaser followed while Bas blundered and bulled his way. He cursed the briars, and said, "So dark down here God needs to pipe in some daylight."

Soon after reaching the juncture of the Yuda and narrow triangle of beargrass that identified the trail he had followed the day before, Obie watched the sun creep above the ridge. It warmed the damp air and designed a surrounding of shadows that shifted with the rhythm of an elusive breeze. Flowing quietly, a dark, deep stretch of the Yuda waited before Obie. To his right meandered the branch creek, the narrow remnant of a trail. He studied the remaining signs of the ancient pathway as if expecting something or someone to emerge from the shadows. He listened, too. Turned his head like a man going deaf. The stillness carried bird songs, rustling leaves and lapping water. The moaning scream that had sent him running from the mysterious valley the previous evening remained hidden on the other side of the ridge.

Bas pointed in the direction Obie looked. "That the direction of the branch you found them pearls on?"

94

"Up over the saddle. There's a valley on the other side." His voice trailed off as he listened intently to all the unfamiliar sounds.

"Seems to me it'd make more sense going back over there than staying here and building this thing you got in your head."

The sun collided with a high gray wall of clouds while they talked. The wind stirred. It frolicked and teased before turning mean. In moments, the overcast gray swirled and boiled into gray-black mold that carried an ominous promise. "Bad weather's a-coming, Obie. That clabbered sky don't look good."

"Then we best get to chopping."

They took turns using the hatchet and skinning the half dozen young basswoods. They used a combination of sorrel and cross-vine to lash the saplings together. "Seems to me," Bas repeated, "it'd make more sense going back over to where you were yesterday. This here contraption ain't gonna hold a one-legged toad."

Rather than a flat-bottomed barge, they pushed a makeshift raft into the river, which Obie intended to ride bareback fashion. "I ain't much on swimming but I can follow along to the sandbar and help you drag that thing back up here if you're fool enough to try it again." He handed Obie a long pole. "Don't you get going too dang fast neither. That's the worst thicket I ever did see. Little feller like you can scoot right along but a feller big as me . . . dang it," Bas said, "just don't get going too durn fast; won't be no way for me to help out if you need it."

"You can hand me the drag line," Obie said, then threw back his head and straightened as a cold shiver stabbed between his shoulder blades. He glanced about as if the pain were some sort of prophetic warning.

"What's ailing you?"

Obie shook his head before turning his attention back to the drag, the five-foot length of poplar. Rocks weighted both ends. Dangling at one-inch intervals along the slender poplar rod were strands of wire Obie had braided together to act as grappling hooks. Before he pushed out toward the center he said, "Bring your knife along, Bas. We'll open the mussels on the sandbar."

"Watch for sucking pots, you hear."

The current caught the raft almost immediately and jerked it crossways in the water. Before Obie lowered the drag, he used the long pole to turn the raft straight with the current and to push himself toward the dark, mysterious center.

Dense thickets of plum trees and sumacs crowded the riverbank. Poplars and magnolias reached out and threw a roof over the river. Obie felt the chilliness in the air, but like so many other signs, he chose to ignore it, too, and pushed the drag off into deep water. He even chose to ignore the sweat on his forehead, the goose bumps that gave him the shivers, the inner voice that cautioned him about the Yuda. But his thoughts and every act focused on finding more pearls . . . finding them without having to return to the mysterious valley over the ridge. And Obie maneuvered the raft farther out into the river.

The current slacked off; it seemed deliberately slow while the deep center took on the look of an ugly old scar. Obie inched the pole down the south side of the raft to keep it straight with the current. Then, to hold it steady, he drove the pole down on the north. It dropped, dropped farther. It continued to drop and Obie lost his balance.

He felt himself falling. He grabbed a handful of air.

His left arm and shoulder, his knee and thigh, slipped into the cold water. He lunged forward. His chest and right shoulder slammed against the basswood logs, while he clutched the pole as it rose to the surface.

Obie crawled back to his knees. The wind cut through the layer of wet clothing and sent a tremor coursing the length of his body. "Damn river," he hissed. "You ain't about to beat me."

He raised onto one foot, then the other. He glanced down at the line and wondered if the grappling hooks were dragging the bottom as he designed them to do. Or was the rope too short?

He shrugged off that possibility but failed to rid himself of the nagging fear that twisted inside his belly. He drove the pole down the north side of the raft, cautiously this time. It touched bottom. Obie eyed the far side of the waterway with suspicion.

"Hey," Bas called from the thicket, "you're a-getting too far ahead. I can't keep up."

"I'll be fine once I hit the sand bar," Obie yelled back. "Where's Chaser?"

Bas disappeared inside a switch-cane brake while a quick series of ripples teetered the raft and made Obie grab for the pole. Was it his imagination or was the river toying with him? Probably had a cussed streak like his brother Virg. And Obie clamped his teeth tight.

No way that Virg was gonna best him this time. Obie already knew the look that would come across his brother's face when he saw the pearls . . . scrunched up, his big eyes squinting, while his brain worked on a way to steal them. Obie grinned; ol' Virg would have to get up awful early to steal his pearls.

The raft quivered as if being drawn toward a cross-current and snatched Obie's thoughts back to the river, which made a slow and wide bend to the southwest. Gravel and chunks of white, milky quartz cluttered both sides of the bank. A ledge jutted out a hundred or so feet above the water. Obie shivered and wished for the coat inside his tow sack. As the raft completed the wide swing, the current increased. The channel narrowed and dipped downhill. Obie poled faster and continuously. He flung the poplar rod from one side of the raft to the other. He knew the danger of not keeping to the center. If he veered to either side, he would miss the sand bar and be carried into the rocky chute. If there was a sucking pot it had to be just ahead of the narrow neck. And the speed of the current doubled, then tripled.

A few yards out from the sandbar, Obie saw the shadow of rocks lurking below the surface. He saw them, but before he could maneuver the raft away, they caught the corner. The basswood logs shot out of the river like a trout, twisting and spinning. The current threw the raft up on its side and Obie off to the south. He caught a handful of switch cane and pulled himself into shallow water. He twisted about . . . the rope? There! He dove for it, caught the end. Rather than retrieving it, the rope drew him out of the shallows and into deeper water. He couldn't let go; he couldn't lose the rope. "Bas! Bas, where are you?"

"Here."

The response came from over Obie's shoulder as Bas's big hands grabbed him, pulled him on to the bank. Together, they drew the crowfoot drag from the current but the raft disappeared.

"You dang near got yourself kilt!" Bas shouted.

"You best sit down and let your breath catch up to you."

Obie pushed back into the switch cane, dropped onto the ground; Chaser licked his cheek but Obie's jaws snapped tight; the grappling lines hung empty. "Dang it! Dang it to pieces."

Bas unloosened the rope from the drag pole. "You ready to start for home now?"

"No. We'll build another raft. It won't take long."

"We ain't building another nothing. Either we're starting for home now or I'll go with you over that saddle to where you found them pearls yesterday."

A cold, stabbing shiver moved down Obie's spine, one vertebra at a time, while memories of voices and shadows filled him with fear.

How could he explain his reluctance to return to the upper valley? He had no proof that something unexplainable hid inside the forest or lurked just below the surface of the branch creek. But did he have a choice? Would Bas's company lessen the risk of something happening?

Obie wrapped his arms tight around his body. He had given his word to leave for home the next day. To accomplish all that he had set out to achieve, he had to find more pearls. Obie knew he had to take the gamble.

CHAPTER
9

* * *

THE MOLDY GRAY-BLACK SKY FILLED THE LONG VALLEY with a gray-green disguise that muted the foliage with its dampish haze. Huddled and pressed together, giant trees stood like silent mourners. Other trees, long ago dead, remained on the fringe, alone and naked, lofty perches now for ravens and buzzards. Every instinct, every shred of common sense advised Obie to turn back. Even a low, distant muttering of thunder rolled over a far ridge to add its warning. Obie closed his eyes. Reasons to leave disputed reasons to stay. They scuffled inside his mind for control, each stirring Obie's deepest fears.

He considered the worst possibility. A severe storm might put their lives in danger, though a flood was unlikely this time of year. Nor did he find rain and high rivers a reason to panic. If he left now, before finding enough pearls to fulfill his dream, his dream would flitter away, the way of most dreams. He would be trapped forever.

For a few minutes he moved easily. He concentrated on finding pearls, on going north, on Chaser pressing against him, on Bas walking behind. But once he started across the clearing of beargrass and switch cane, he felt the unseen presence float in upon him.

The cane hissed against his pant legs; a faint breeze rattled dried leaves; other sounds, scarcely perceptible, crowded into the silence. Obie's imagination reawakened. It supplied a threat behind every tree, inside every patch of dense fog. Was the threat a man—a Cherokee? A Nun Yuna Wi? One of the Immortals? Obie listened to the questions rattle inside his mind. He felt helpless to still them. He tried reasoning with himself; ghosts and spirits were superstition and if he doubted that, then he must search every corner and crevice of the valley, force the Nun Yuna Wi to show himself, challenge him the way his daddy called out the spirit from the ashes of Granddaddy Claiborne's cabin. But such a search required time. And he had given his word to leave for home come morning. At best only a few more hours remained to find enough pearls to make his dream happen.

"This here is the most still place I ever seen." Bas moved up alongside. "Quiet like a burying yard."

Obie shuddered as he dropped his tow sack alongside the creek. "I'll start working above the rapids. Biggest pearl I found came from that stretch. From there I'll move south, a quarter mile or so." Obie ran his hand along Chaser's spine. "You coming along or you going to look for that deer I saw yesterday?"

"Ain't much I kin help do since you just brung that one rope. I'll take Chaser. We're sure to scare up something." Bas studied the lay of things. "Think I'll cut up that a-way. If I can't find you along the branch, I'll fire my rifle real fast together."

"I won't be long," Obie said. "It's gonna get dark in a hurry come evening. Might even storm."

Obie left behind everything—shoes, socks, coat—taking only the knife and grappling line. He waved, set off upstream. Twice he glanced back to reassure himself of Bas's presence and twice he stifled the temptation to whistle for his dog. It was true, they did need meat to fill their empty bellies and to get them home. But as each step carried him farther from Chaser, Bas and the rifle, Obie felt the frightful certainty that something was wrong. It stretched and knotted every muscle in his body. A bitter taste set his teeth on edge.

"Lord," Obie said, "I didn't come here just for myself. The real reason for me needing so many pearls is to pay off my daddy's debts. I can't believe that a few extra for myself is going against Your will. It says in the Good Book, *'the Lord helps them that helps themselves.'* " Obie ran his tongue across his lips. "That's all I'm doing, Lord, just trying to improve myself. And I can do that if You'll just help me to get up north and better myself like You helped Uncle Tully."

The pounding inside Obie's chest grew as he followed the steep incline beyond the rapids to where the ground leveled. Wind designed momentary ripples across slow-moving green-black water. The truth of the creek and mysterious valley remained hidden, while some deep instinct within Obie broke through the wall of prophetic inspiration to warn him. He shivered. He sensed someone watching. But who was out there? Blood wheezed in his ears and thickened his tongue. Yet he continued on until reaching that place where the forest touched the creek.

An inlay of dark and light shadows hovered above the water. Poplars, locust and sweetgums encroached upon the stream while the wide and deceivingly slow-moving body flowed beneath a coverlet of dead limbs and dried leaves. He stared at the impossible tangle of vines, shrubs and saplings along the water's edge.

The thought of wading into the current to throw the line belched up a troubled sigh that escaped his lips. He rubbed his forehead and the ache that thumped inside. Another ache chewed at his brain, and if he let his mind run free, he just might bawl.

Obie turned his back on the tangled thicket, on the idea of continuing ahead, on his desire for more and larger pearls. He saw several nearby places to throw out the grappling line. All looked equally promising. He studied the sites carefully, yet an inner craving argued against the merit of each and pulled him to go on.

"Nope," Obie hissed and swung around to examine the thicket. He swore, too, at his craving for more and larger pearls and every thought that pushed him to go deeper into the forested valley. Never in his life could he remember being so divided. He wanted to go north; he surely did. He needed the additional pearls to make it happen, yet the forest and the mysteriousness that lay inside its dark and protective cover scared him.

"How come?" Obie shouted. "How come You have to make everything so hard? How come, Lord?"

Obie glared at the dense wall. "Well, You'll not stop me!" And he set out to challenge the thicket.

He used his body like a ram and bulled his way past

the outer fringe. Trees roofed the forest, shut out the hazy sunlight. They held in the cool and all the smells of wet earth, living plants and decay. They concealed shadows. They hid the creators of so many puzzling sounds.

Each bit of ground he gained led him into a more impossible snarl. It forced him to his knees, to crawl like a shrew. He hated being insignificant; he hated things bigger and more powerful than he was. The energy of that hatred thrust him on.

Minutes wasted away, using up an hour or more. He noticed red streaks crisscrossing the backs of his hands. Those same red streaks showed on his arms where his shirt was torn away and he felt an itch on the back of his neck. Hunger tormented him but the obsession to go north, to put Virg Wilks out of his life forever, gave him the energy to continue. Though his thoughts seethed with anger, Obie remained alert to the creek and its tell-tale sounds. He paused often to listen. A faint gurgling caused him to veer left until, through the maze of green-ery, he picked out patches of murky green-black water. Satisfied, yet driven to find that one special spot on the creek, free of all entanglements, Obie moved ahead.

He dismissed the ache in his belly, his swelling hands and blurred vision. He dismissed the sweat, the fire blaz-ing up inside him. He dismissed everything except the pearls that waited for the taking.

"Lawdy, Jehovah!" Obie sucked in his breath. He stopped dead. Like a frightened creature, he peered from behind an overlay of leaves and branches into a sun-brightened clearing. He blinked several times, shook his head to clear away the dizziness.

"Ain't so," he muttered. "I'm dreaming this."

He crawled quietly and carefully through the thinning outer fringe, yet chose to remain hidden. He sat back on his heels. His mind contradicted the spectacle before him. "Not so," he said again. Yet rising up from the center of an unexplainable circular clearing, he saw a round mound . . . a heap of dirt bigger than any house in Graysonia.

Obie rubbed his eyes but no amount of rubbing erased the vision. The mound remained. Beyond it lay the creek, and the open, grassy-green bank he knew he would find. The excitement of finding it thrust him ahead. But the immense mound and all of its foreboding pulled him back to his hiding place. Obie felt a slow, painful tearing inside his brain. He tried to still his fear; *the pearls waited!* More than he could possibly imagine. He knew it.

Before leaving the security of the forest, Obie searched the clearing for a sign of someone else. Satisfied that nothing two-legged or otherwise waited to gobble him up, he crawled out, crawled backward toward the faint sounds of water seeping downstream.

Obie looked beyond the sun, the lacy collar of haze that softened its brightness. "Thank you, Lord," he whispered, unloosened the rope from around his middle, turned and faced the creek.

A sheer rock wall held in the flow on the opposite side. The wall reached to the dividing ridge and gave shape to the seemingly still water. As Obie moved closer, he listened for the sound of birds, for anything familiar. But it was only the wind and forest that stirred amid the stifling odor of earth and decay.

Could this be the place Micager Wilks found the mussel beds, the place of the sucking pot and the underwater cave? Obie examined the far rock wall for signs of an opening. If such a cave existed, Obie thought, the entrance must be hidden below the water's surface. But he saw no evidence of it, and after attaching a rock weight to the line, he heaved it toward the opposite side.

Would Bas be able to find him? He had gone much farther than a quarter of a mile. Would he be able to hear Bas's signal? Obie walked upstream a short distance. Would he be able to get back before dark? He considered building a signal fire but the wind blew out of the northwest and would carry the smoke off in the opposite direction. Obie pulled on the line. He knew by the feel that the wires were full. "Hot-dang-daddy," he shouted and drew the line onto the grassy bank.

He stripped the wires and returned the line to the creek. It sank below the mirrored surface, which flowed parallel with the rock wall. Rather than leaving the mussels to open later, Obie sank to his knees. He mistrusted the ever-darkening sky and his ability to find his way back quickly.

"Yowieee!" The excitement in his voice shot into the sky and all his fears were forgotten.

Each mussel produced a beautiful petal-pink pearl of at least ten grains. Obie added eight of them to the packet from inside his pocket, which he returned and securely fastened. With his finger still twisting the button, he glanced back at the mound.

All part of the old days, he told himself. Nothing to fret over now. But his mind refused to let go. Hidden beneath tons of earth rested the remains of men, women and children, all they owned, all they used in their daily lives. Would their pearls have been buried with them? He suspected so. How many? How big? But most of all, where was the Indian who survived the last burial?

Obie shivered as he worked the line in, hand over hand. Again, he knew by the feel of it that the wires held a sizeable catch. He laughed. He thought about Bas and what he would say, then about Virg. His brother would hook his thumbs in the straps of his overalls, wrinkle his face into a *who cares* kind of look; he'd say something sappy like, "Ain't much to show for the time you been gone."

"Maybe not," Obie said aloud, "but it's sure gonna get me away from you. You'll not ever again get the chance to bloody my nose."

Obie stripped the wires and returned the line to the creek. Water splashed, fell back and became part of the circular wake that appeared to flow opposite the current.

Obie studied the peculiarity, then shrugging, attributed it to another of the creek's mysteries and dropped to his knees to open the mussels. Though he knew it was only a notion of his imagination, he glanced over at the mound, feeling hundreds of eyes watching and condemning him. In the minds of those buried there, he must be no better than De Soto or the other Spaniards who came to steal their pearls. Was this creek one of the waterways the explorers followed? Before Obie decided, a sharp, guttural sound burst from inside the forest. He drew back his knife; he inched his gaze from left to right, admitted to himself that it could have been a wild turkey rather than some sort of boogerish predator.

Wild turkey roasted over hot coals . . . Obie moaned aloud, then laughed a happy sound. Nothing better than biting into a chunk of hot juicy meat. But he found another pearl, petal-pink, then several more. Not only was the pain in his belly forgotten but the burying mound and his other curious notions disappeared, too. He even dismissed the sharp, harsh, guttural sound as it moved closer.

But he did wish for a gun, then admitted to being a terrible shot. Mrs. Middleton once sent a note home, suggesting that his mamma have his eyes looked at. Mrs. Middleton didn't know Delsie had to stuff cardboard squares inside her shoes to cover the holes; Josh didn't have a winter coat. And Obie was wearing Virg's worn-out overalls. Wasn't fair. He was the oldest; new clothes should be bought for him, not his younger brother.

Obie raised from his knees, added seven more pearls to his collection, before pushing the packet to the bottom of his pocket and buttoning it carefully. He'd not lose the pearls nor have to wear anybody's hand-me-downs ever again. Especially Virg's.

As Obie wiped his sticky, smelly hands down the sides of his overalls, he felt a strange stiffness in his fingers. They were swollen and little red bumps looked like freckles up his arms. Poison ivy? He didn't think so. He had gotten into weeds before, made him itch but never dizzy or feverish. And Obie swayed from the effects of both.

Wind and its growing chill prompted him to gather wood and build a fire. Soon it blazed up and its warmth followed him to the water's edge, where he drew in the line another time. He removed a dozen more ripplebacks. Rather than opening them, he set them on a rock near the fire and moved farther south to a place where the water looked deepest, then threw out the line.

He tied off the end to a sapling, then returned to

the fire, to the comfort of its crackling. The sound kept him from hearing other sounds. The smell of smoke kept him from smelling the air's growing dampness. As Obie began opening the ripplebacks, he thought about the north, living in a place of his own, sleeping in a bed by himself. Someday he'd even have enough money to buy his own automobile. He'd have himself a white suit and shoes to match. He'd bring his mamma more than toilet water when he came to visit; a new dress maybe and a box of fancy chocolates for the younguns.

Thunder? No . . . rifle fire.

"Dang it," Obie yelled, "I bet you just shot us that turkey, Bas Allardice. Maybe even a deer."

Obie drove the sharp, thick bladed knife between the seam and pried the shells apart. It took several seconds for him to focus his eyes on the open mussel.

A baroque? Bigger than a black-eyed pea! He counted sixty-seven and then added the baroque to his collection.

He gave an excited yell of happiness, of relief, of great expectancy. But his joy subsided when, from the corner of his eye, he noticed the sapling bend toward the water. The line snapped tight across the creek and pulled the sapling flat. It tossed and twisted and bucked like something alive worked the hidden end. Whatever it was partially uprooted the sapling and drew it into shallow water.

Obie rose slowly. He stood with unsteady legs and squinted in hopes of improving his vision. The fast-moving current threatened to sweep away his line. Obie bolted ahead; he ran along the bank and into shallow water. When within an arm's reach of the rope, he saw it go limp. It lay still, snakelike across the dark, mirrored surface.

He studied it, waited for it to move. Twice he reached out to grab it. Twice he drew back empty handed. He watched the current move, yet the rope remained still as if suspended, a hair's width, above the watery surface. Seconds passed. A silence, so still, caused his breathing to boom inside the hush. Obie dropped down, his body swollen and awkward. He inched his hand ahead, then with suspicious fingers he cautiously took hold of the rope.

It lay lifeless across his palm. He moistened his lips; he did not intend to be jerked into the water and swept away. Standing and with measured steps, he closed his hand around the rope. He stepped back through the shallow apron and up onto the bank, where he looked down into the center of the creek.

Shadows, submerged rocks and vegetation, caught on sunken debris, looked back at him. His gaze crept slowly toward the opposite side. But the water darkened and made it impossible to see more than lines and shadows.

A burst of wind whipped through the forest, across the water and twisted his hair over his eyes. Obie flipped his head and hair aside. He blinked. He blinked several more times, questioning what he saw. It appeared to be a man, resting on his side, bent in a half circle. Then it dissolved into a gnarled tree, wearing moss and rotting vegetation. Of course it had to be the latter, but before he could quiet the tremor causing his hands to quiver, a long and hollow scream rose from out of the forest. The sort of sound someone might make when falling from a high place.

Bas? Obie spun on his heels but the burying mound reared up to block his view. To the north and south the forest's long arms reached to the sky. The same howling cry rose again and cut through the cold air, but this time, a louder cry from a closer distance responded.

The cries froze Obie to the earth. His heart shot so high into his throat, he felt it press against his windpipe and threaten to choke him. Bas? No. A cat, then? Would a wild boar make such a hideous noise? A bear roared. But a wolf howled . . . so—so did a man.

Obie tried to see in every direction as the howling cry continued in the south and rolled around the perimeter of the mound. It soared to a higher and higher pitch. It hung in the stillness like fog, then softened and disappeared. The wind? "Not likely!" he said as panic swept through him.

His blood turned cold and thick. His body, partially paralyzed, moved in slow motion only. With his gaze locked over the belly of the mound, he backed off until the creek halted his retreat. Nor could he escape the hatred his mind envisioned coming from the interior of the mound. Fired by that hatred, the open space between the mound and creek became a griddle and just at the edge of Obie's vision, a shimmering mirage boiled out of the earth and sent an incomprehensible foreboding coursing through his body.

The legend was true! The Nun Yuna Wi existed. It wasn't just story talk. Wind buffeted him from the side and churned the water into agitated waves that rolled and bucked against both banks. *The Nun Yuna Wi existed.*

To this day they lived and moved through the hills that surrounded him. What did their presence mean to his safety, to his return home? Obie stared at the mound, at the layer of clouds sinking over the hills and obscuring the upper reaches. It would be dark long before he made his way back through the thicket where Bas and Chaser waited.

Feeling the sudden urgency, Obie pulled on the rope. But something unseen held the submerged end. Obie jerked. He jerked harder. His foot slipped on mossy rocks and he went down. Rather than releasing the line, he tried to save it and the mussels he knew would be locked over the wires. He struggled to his knees, pulled against the unseen force. By planting a heel, he thrust his body up and drew back. He should let go; he knew he should; he had enough pearls. Yet he continued to hold on, continued to think his strength superior. He held on until he smashed headlong into the current. As he came up from the bottom, gasping, he recognized the smell of smoke, clouds swirling overhead, the feel of icy wind against his face. Then the current spun him and took him deeper, to where gravel-sized rocks whirled like marbles.

Obie kicked at the water. He took in great armfuls. He grabbed at submerged boulders, but each time his fingers left deep furrows through the mossy slick surface as they slipped away. And the current reclaimed him, to toss him about at will, to twist the grappling line more tightly about him.

Obie planted his toes in the soft bottom and lunged for the shallows. He clawed at the muddy bottom to hold his momentary advance while the pull against his legs lessened for a brief instant.

The urge to yell burst past his lips. *He was safe.* His hand shot up to his pocket. *The pearls were safe, too.* But the soft mud gradually gave way. No amount of struggling saved him from the current. It whipped him about. It turned him inside the grappling line and made escape impossible.

Obie flung himself one way, then the other. Each time he resurfaced, he took deep gulps of air to refill his stinging lungs. He saw the bank; maybe fifteen feet away now, but the undertow and its invisible power sucked him deeper.

Before his head sank beneath the surface, Obie yelled for help, not because he expected Bas to hear but because the effort released the ever-building panic welling inside his mind.

As the creek bed stepped down, a succession of steep, rough rapids waited. Their sound loudened. The stream bed shrank into a swirling, narrow funnel. If he were to survive, he must keep to the center. He flailed at the water. He maneuvered toward the channel. But the current sucked him against the rock wall and down into its murky blackness. Wild fright exploded inside him as the current surged with a crossways action and threw him in circles. His arms ached from the struggle; his legs quivered; a sense of helplessness stole his ability to reason.

He knew he was crying even though water soaked up the sounds. He knew he was going to drown, too. Some distance ahead, he saw a light made yellow-green by murky vapors. Obie's chest burst as the current pounded him against moss-slick walls. It drew him deeper, continued to spin him in circles, to batter his shoulders and ribs against the graybacks. He flipped upside down, struck his head and felt something inside let go.

A silence so still made him wonder if he was dead.

Dead? What was dead? He floated beneath the surface peacefully and moved with the current through calm waters. He recognized the undersides of leaves bobbing overhead, debris and the mossy vegetation it carried along. If he was dead, how could he continue to think?

But the peaceful interlude ended as a furious rush of water flung him around a wheel of stinging sounds. One peal after another of deafening thunder knifed through the water. A part of him, like some sort of underwater creature, watched his body being thrown against the wall. His head rolled in unnatural ways and he suspected his neck was broken. He suspected, too, that this furious force holding him down was the same Untigubi that Micager Wilks told about—a sucking pot that took live men into its vortex before spitting out corpses.

As Obie settled deeper into the vortex, the grappling line fell from around him. His arms hung limp and useless. His legs dangled, even his brain lacked the energy to resist, content to observe, and he slipped inside a narrowing rock tunnel. One flash of light after another revealed granite walls, the spout of a funnel. Something pulled on Obie's feet. It sucked him down through the spout, then spit him out into a pool of crystal clear water deep inside the mountain's belly.

The water felt cool against his stinging hot skin, soothing, almost medicinal. Stalactites hung from overhead. Rain-freshened air filled the emptiness and Obie took deep gulps of it. Was this the cave of the giant pigtoe, the home of the stone man, the Nun Yuna Wi, the Immortals?

Was he dead?

Before he guessed at an answer, a faint moaning caused Obie to wrench around. He blinked several times, held his breath to hear more clearly. The sound sharpened, grew more distinct. It moved slowly closer. Its nearness sent shivers through him. His fear turned to panic. When it turned to horror, he cried out, leaving the sound of his terror on every vaporous droplet to vibrate inside the belly again and again and again.

Stepping out of the gray mist, a shapeless but glowing form stared at Obie. Was this a Nun Yuna Wi? One of the Immortals? It was a form without eyes or ears, nose or mouth, yet it glowed like sunlight.

A shapeless arm reached for Obie. He pushed back. He covered his pocket and the packet of pearls with both hands. "They're mine," he shouted. "I found them. They're mine now."

The arm caught hold of him. It drew him up into a place of white light and moist warm air.

Was he dead? Was this heaven?

Cabins stretched across a fertile cove and up hillsides. Fields lay green with corn and barley. Bridges crossed creeks; cows grazed on grass; orchards stood ripe with fruit; villagers, glowing and formless, waved as Obie stepped from the mountain's belly. They called him by name. Someone small smiled without smiling, laughed without sound, spoke without words and took Obie by the hand to walk in air scented with pine pitch and roasting meat. People invited him to eat—sweet potato tubers, stewed apples, corn, venison, wild turkey, sweet honey. While he ate, other villagers, strangely alike in their glowing brilliance, waited to invite him to share their hospitality. They offered wordless praise and told silent stories. They encouraged him to dance and play games, to help with their chores and work in their fields.

Obie consumed all they offered before he stretched

flat on a pile of sweet-smelling grass and slept. He dreamt pleasantly at first, but the longer he slept and the more separated he became, the more disturbing his dreams.

Hands reached for him. Instead of welcoming ones, they came at him with clutching fingers, demanding the pearls from his pocket. Obie shook his head. He batted their hands aside. But there were too many and he lost control. He yelled at them, screamed at them to go away—

"Obie," Bas shouted, "wake up. Wake up, you hear."

Smoke stung his eyes; burning pine splinters irritated his nostrils; wind, cold and icy, whipped down upon him. "Obie." Bas shook him by the shoulders. "You got anything broke? Wake up, Obie."

Obie opened his eyes. *Where were they?* He squeezed his eyes shut. *There!* His eyes popped open; he pulled back, pulled free of Bas's hold, pulled into himself. *There, lined up and waiting.*

"Obie." Bas shook him a second time. "What's ailing you? We ain't got time to waste. We got to get shed of this place. Obie, you hear me?"

The demanding hands and clutching fingers changed into Bas's troubled face. Firelight danced inside his narrowed eyes while wind howled down out of the trees and carried the scent of roasting meat. "Lawdy, Obie, I near give you up for dead. If it weren't for this here turkey a-cooking, I would have hightailed it outta this place long before now. Obie, you hearing me?"

Obie lifted up onto an elbow, fell back and groaned. Pain pushed out from inside his body. Chaser licked his cheek, his ears, and only stopped because Obie brushed her aside. Again he raised up. He peered into the darkness, saw outlines obscured by a thickening gray haze, asked, "Where am I?"

"You telling me you don't know?"

Obie heard the creek. He listened to the wind. He smelled pine pitch, Chaser's wet fur, turkey, and the sticky nacre. Yet his lips were sweet with the taste of wild honey.

He turned his face into the cold hoping to clear the heaviness from inside his head. "The pearls!" He twisted around. A pain stabbed between his ribs yet he shoved his hand into the pocket. "I was afraid they might have stolen them. They tried. They were after me." Obie paused as he tried to sort through the facts. *The Nun Yuna Wi . . . the Immortals . . .* "I saw people; not people like you or me. They . . . they were . . ." *They had given him food, talked, but all the while they had been after his pearls.*

Obie recognized the questioning turn upon Bas's lips. "How did you find me. I fell in—"

Fell in? Obie tried to remember: *Fell in or was he pulled?* He sat cross-legged before the fire, took his coat from around his shoulders and slipped into it. "It was far back in the valley where it happened," he explained. "A half mile maybe."

"Can you walk, Obie?"

"How did you find me?"

"I didn't; you come shooting down them rapids like a windmill gone bad. Chaser got to you before I did. Can you walk?"

Obie held his hands to the fire. The knuckles were scraped raw, but the red and swollen skin had vanished. Slowly the fuzziness lifted from his vision.

"You got the biggest, sorriest looking pump-knot on

117

your head I ever did see. Can you walk? We need to be leaving this here place. It's gonna rain pitchforks and bull yearlings."

Obie pulled his shoes and socks from the tow sack. Lightning flashed in the northwest. He slipped into the shoes and tied the laces while Bas wrapped his smoke-browned turkey inside the tow sack. Obie tried to stand, dropped back to his knees.

"We gotta get away from this place, Obie. These woods is full of panthers and catamounts. I seen their track all over the place, heard them squalling in the pineries, too."

Obie took Bas's arm and pulled up onto his feet. His knees gave a bit but Bas caught him before he went down. "This here is a strange place, Obie. Not like home country."

Obie looked out into the darkness. Hands reached from the creek's murky waters. They grabbed for him; they wanted their pearls. "We have to hurry, Bas. They'll be after us."

"Obie—"

But Obie stumbled into the darkness and whatever it offered.

CHAPTER

10

* * *

THOUGH HIS LEGS WERE SHORTER AND HIS STRIDE LESS, OBIE stayed a half dozen steps ahead of Bas as they picked their way to the saddle, then down the other side. Obie's pulse drummed inside his head, like a blacksmith pounding on an anvil. And he glanced back over his shoulder more than once. He whistled for Chaser to catch up or called out to Bas. But neither was the cause for his looking back. He knew the Nun Yuna Wi were following. He felt their presence as surely as he felt the wet clothes sticking to his body. He knew they wanted his pearls, that they would destroy him to get them. He suspected, too, that he had not seen the last of the Nun Yuna Wi. They were out there . . . waiting.

He kept telling himself he was lucky to be alive, lucky to have escaped the sucking pot in one piece. But had it been just luck? Or had the Immortals spit him out because he had something more to do with his life?

Each step that took Obie closer to home, took him closer to that place called Michigan, to why the Immortals had spared him. But he didn't expect the Nun Yuna Wi to give up, to just let him go because the Immortals saw that he had something important to do with his life. And the day's happenings became shadows that continued to jump out at him from the dark.

While waiting for Bas to catch up and before striking off on the hour-long walk back to the cave, Obie turned in a slow circle. "You're out there," he whispered. "I know you are. I know you're after my pearls, too, but you'll not have them. You don't need them bad as I do."

Wind came off the river and whipped against him. Its cold fingers turned him numb and he hugged his tow sack tight to his belly to hold off the chill.

"I feel rain," Bas called, moving down the hill. "It's gonna be a real thunder-buster." Bas pulled even. Stopped. "Obie, nobody wants down outta these here hills worse than me, but you got something eating on you that you ain't told me. What happened to you? What's making you so skittish?"

"I'm not skittish. I'm cold," Obie fired back. "Let's get."

But Bas caught Obie's arm and refused to let go. "Something happened to you in that branch, didn't it? Did you see a booger? Is that what we got chasing after us?"

"Shut up about boogers." Obie's temper flared. "Let's get. Rain won't hold off forever."

"Reckon you're right about that." Bas stepped in front and pushed his tow sack, with the turkey inside, into Obie's arms. "Going so fast in the dark ain't wisdom; good way to twist a leg. I'll be breaking trail for a ways, and don't you be losing my turkey. Come morning," Bas added, "you'll be empty as a pig trough, same as me."

With the Yuda on his right, Bas hugged to the water's edge. "Being wet," he called back, "is a whole lot better than tangled up in the poison ivy."

Obie wanted to argue with Bas's reason. He wanted to argue about being pushed to the back and Bas's slower pace. "Chaser," he called, "you stay close up front so you can warn us if something's sneaking in to have us for supper."

A low and constant muttering of thunder rolled out of the northwest while brief flashes of lightning showered across the forest with splinters of silver-blue light. When Bas reached that part of the river where the thicket became an almost impossible snarl, he moved farther into the water.

"What are you doing?" Obie yelled, feeling the increased pull of the current against his legs. "There are sucking pots out here; we might stumble and get caught up in the current."

Bas, a dark shadow in the night, stopped. "You forgetting I been up and down this river bank a time or two? How you figure I got to you so quick when you fell off that contraption you was a-riding? I was in the river, that's how." Bas paused to catch his breath. "Folks say us Allardices ain't never walked far with Solomon. But that ain't altogether true. Maybe we ain't took to schooling like you but that don't mean we is stupid. Not a one of us Allardices was born behind the barn."

Water sloshed inside Obie's shoes and reached to his knees. Hot sweat ran from his face, causing him to shiver. "I'm sorry," he said. "I'm plumb wore out."

The river and wind carried off Bas's response, leaving Obie angry, feeling guilty besides. "Chaser," he called. "Chaser, where the devil are you? Chaser!"

The dog nudged him with her nose.

"You stay close by. If you don't and you get in trouble, I can't help."

Clouds dropped down and filled the hollow, turning the air into a wet mist that soaked Obie's hair and ran into his eyes. He shifted the weight of the tow sack on his shoulder. "Hurry it up, Bas. It's so dang dark I can't see to the other side of the river."

Silently, Obie cried out for the warmth of a fire and a quilt to roll up inside. His body burned with fatigue. His mind twisted every tree branch, every leaf into the Nun Yuna Wi. Obie wanted to yell. He raised his hand to his pocket instead. Feeling the pearls eased the knot in his belly and allowed him time to think.

Again he told himself that his escape from the sucking pot was no accident. He believed that, felt it in his gut. It would be his destiny to go north, make something of himself like his uncle Tully had done. Yet the idea of his having a special destiny and his wish for it to be true failed to eliminate his fear of the night and all the terrors it held. The Nun Yuna Wi didn't give a tinker's damn about his destiny; they wanted their pearls! And his mind ran on like his mamma's Big Ben alarm clock.

. . . going north, going north, going north . . . working a paying job . . . spending money rattling inside my pockets . . . buying things instead of doing without . . . food to eat more than what a feller can grow . . . sleeping in my own bed in a room all to myself . . . new clothes . . . shoes without holes . . . polish for shining them instead of stove soot . . . store-bought laces instead of string . . . oranges . . .

Inside Obie's head images spun in a slow circle; his eyelids flapped open and shut like loose shingles. He smelled tree-ripened oranges, felt the sticky wet on his fingers, saw the two halves fall apart, all glistening and bright. He sank his teeth into the first half, sucked up the juice, the oily fragrance all the way to his brain, rolled the sweetness around inside his mouth and only swallowed the pulp when every bit of flavor was gone. Licked his chin and nose, greedy for the last juicy dribble and smudge.

Obie pressed his tongue against the back of his teeth, feeling the pulp lodged between the two big front ones. He reached up with a finger to help. "Dang!" he muttered, thinking how real it seemed.

He continued to smell oranges. The orange-colored oil sweeted his fingertips, even his nostrils. He took in deep breaths, trying to force the scent through his body and into every pore. Instead, the wet air pushed beneath his skin, into the pit of his stomach and intensified the ache that moved into every part of his body.

Raising his gaze through the trees, Obie blinked aside the mist. The sky wore a strange appearance, like a pile of smoldering gray-black coals preparing to explode. Lightning broke overhead while the following clap of thunder ricocheted off the ridge tops and rolled down the hollow. "I need Your help in getting these pearls to home. I'm feeling poorly, like the grippe's waiting for me off there in the shadows with the Nun Yuna Wi. They're after me. They want my pearls."

"What's that you're a-saying?" Bas pulled Obie from the water and grabbed his tow sack. "Cave's right down there."

"We made it?" Obie asked. "We made it!"

Bas raised the rifle to his shoulder. "Let's get on down outta here before the storm hits. It's gonna be a booger." Bas pushed his face closer to Obie's. "If you ain't up to walking, I can tote you."

Obie laughed. "Last one down's a ruptured duck."

Wind boiled over the ridge top and into the hollow. It swirled inside the cove as it sought a channel of escape. "Dang!" Bas yelled, as droplets of rain quickly turned into slashes of water.

But it stopped by the time they reached the ledge. Chaser shook herself. Bas tossed the tow sacks aside and set a fire with wood he had stored at the back of the cave. It flared up brilliantly, almost instantly, but Obie was too tired to ask why.

"I feel like I outta be hung out to dry," Bas said and banged his hat against his leg. "Pull off them sopping duds, you hear. Soon as I fetch water from the spring, I'll boil up some coffee to drink with my turkey."

Obie dug the packet of pearls from his overall pocket and set it aside before stripping to his hide. He wrapped up inside his quilt and Bas's, too. He spread his clothes to dry. He hugged close to the bright orange flames that ate through the tepee of dried kindling. "Chaser, come here, girl."

Obie snapped his fingers before retrieving the packet of pearls from the ground. He held it to the light, studied the piece of flannel fabric torn from the tail of his shirt, and thought about the pearls inside. "Look at these, Chaser. Look what we're gonna take home to Mamma. She's gonna be so happy. I can hear her laughing, thanking the Lord and swearing that Mr. Arvis Cagley would skin a mouse for its hide and tallow." Obie laughed. "She might even take on a kind streak, Chaser, and let you sleep under the stove a night or two."

But would her kind streak extend to wishing him well when she learned of his plan? Would she accept that he had a destiny of his own? What would she do to try and keep him home? Stop talking, call him a selfish no-account, threaten him with the wrath of God? Obie slumped forward. He rubbed his nose against the quilt that covered his arms. His nostrils flared as he caught the scent of earth and pine pitch.

He had found sixty-eight pearls. Thirty-four of them were his. His great-granddaddy's map, River Country, finding pearls hadn't been a pie-in-the-sky kind of idea after all. But now he had to get the pearls home. He could no longer remember the number of days he had been away, or the days left before his daddy's note came due. Finding pearls had obsessed him. Why did the dangers of getting them home in time now seep into his thoughts and fill him with dread?

Obie jerked straight. He shook himself. He stared into the fire. He wanted to sleep but each time he closed his eyes, he felt the pull of the unknown.

Obie cupped his hands behind his head and straightened his spine. If he had been knocked unconscious in that river, then the Immortals, the sucking pot, the Nun Yuna Wi were the same as dreams. Dreams were nothing to fear. He reasoned, too, that if Micager Wilks's map got him to River Country, then it would get him home. Yet why did his belly feel so stuffed full of food? What happened to the red splotches up and down his arms? Why could he still taste wild honey on his lips? Obie looked beyond the fire into the dark that filled the cave's entrance.

Night swallowed up everything, everything except the storm. Wind rushed over the northerly ridge, hissed through the trees and down the steep incline. It jumped the river and swirled up the cove. It struck the ledge and shot skyward, sucking up grit and granite particles, lifting the hair along Chaser's back; it tossed Obie's wet clothes into a heap. It uprooted trees and broke limbs. In the wake of the tempest, lightning set the dark ablaze with ghostly silver-white webs. The whole night and all the terror held inside its thunderous blackness seemed bent on destroying him.

Obie closed his eyes. *Every muscle ached; not a joint that wasn't shivering cold; drums banged inside his head; sparks crackled in his ears.* Obie longed for home, a night's sleep in his mamma's feather bed and a dose of her laudanum.

"I'm a-telling you, Obie, it's boogerish out there." Bas set the kettle of water over the fire and glanced at Obie in a curious way. "We got meat for a day, this here cave for as long as we need, but what's troubling me is getting ourselves to the other side of the Sallapoosa. Can't decide if it's wisdom to wait out the storm or head for home. Heavy rain'll turn the river fierce for days. And you ain't got days if you're fixing to pay Arvis Cagley before the first of the month."

Bas sucked in his cheeks. "Obie, you hearing me?"

He nodded but other sounds occupied Obie's thoughts. He strained to see beyond the dark opening, to distinguish the wind and its furor from the eerie sucking. Thunder rang in his ears. His memory of the Nun Yuna

Wi sent his mind rushing ahead. Finally Obie responded: "There's no way we can get back to the Sallapoosa in the dark. It's too far and dangerous. You said so yourself."

"I know what I said." Bas pushed back his hat and scratched his head. "It's no more than an hour's walk."

"But there's a storm coming. You're crazy."

"Crazy?" Bas rocked back and forth on his heels. "I been telling you for two days that a storm were brewing. How come you to act like you just heared it?"

A quiet fell between them, a time to exchange glances and consider. "When you was over that next ridge, you couldn't wait to get back to this here cave. Now that you're here, you're acting like you're skeered to leave."

"I can't go another step. I near gave out that last ways back," Obie defended. "And you haven't said what we'll do when we get to the river."

Once again the same quiet rose between them, allowing time for Obie's reasons to be reshaped into excuses. "It's good to be skeered," Bas said. "Might save you from rushing across that river the way you done getting here."

"I'm not scared." Obie felt a cold spasm vibrate down his spine.

"You know," Bas said, "I never liked you very much. You was too uppity to my liking . . . just like your uncle Tully. But Tully Crumpler never done nothing for nobody." Bas broke a twig from a dead length of chestnut and slipped it between his lips. "Damn," Bas said, around the twig wedged between his teeth, "I ain't never gonna do good with words."

Bas squatted on his heels. He used the twig from between his teeth to point at Obie. "It's time to pack up and get. Don't matter if you're poorly, cold, even dying. Before this here night is over we'll be lucky to be in one piece."

"Then let's wait . . . just until morning. We'll be safe here."

"Safe? Safe from what?"

When Obie refused to reply, Bas said, "If we wait the rain's sure to swell the river, put it over its bank, run every bit of game to high ground. Obie, it's stay here and starve or move on."

"It's not raining now. It's over. You'll see."

"Over? Sounds like that knock you took to your head has addled your brains." Bas gathered Obie's clothes from the back of the cave and dropped them at his feet. "I'm fixing to leave here and I'm taking you along, either on them feet you got or over my shoulder. Makes me no never mind which way it is neither. Ain't gonna give your mamma cause to say no more bad things about us Allardices."

"Bas, I can scarcely put one foot ahead of the other."

Bas stood quiet a few seconds before he said, "Your brother told me I'd be sorry for coming along. He told me you got a yellow streak broad as an axe handle. Reckon he knowd you good."

Obie watched the flames lick around the dead limbs until they caught on fire. He saw his brother's face, the smirk that drew his thick lips back into a tight smile. Slowly, Obie pulled up. He threw both quilts aside. "You can believe what my brother says if you got a mind, but he's the biggest liar that was ever born. Besides that, he's lower than a tumble bug!"

Obie yanked his overalls up from the floor of the

cave. "You still haven't said what we're gonna do if we get to the river. Crossing it in the dark will be harder than putting butter under a wildcat's tail."

"If that's what it takes, we'll do it."

"You're crazy," Obie shouted. "Crazy as Elvira Blackledgee's half-sister."

CHAPTER

11

∗ ∗ ∗

OBIE WORKED HIS LEGS INTO DAMP OVERALLS. HE PULLED ON a wet sock and jerked it over his heel. The top stretched. The heel tore. He ripped the sock from his foot, threw it into the fire. "This idea of yours is going to get us dead. There's no way we can cross the Sallapoosa in the dark. Was scary enough when we could see."

Bas looked down while firelight reached up and ignited bright sparks in his blue eyes. The eyes narrowed in thoughtfulness, then widened and intensified in their knowing. "Virg is right again, you are an aggravation. Don't know why I'm a-bothering with you."

The indifference in Bas's voice caused Obie to turn away from the webs of lightning outside, to examine the furrows of loose flesh across Bas's forehead. He wanted to lash back at Bas, admit he was afraid, but deny he was a pain. He wanted to call Bas stupid, a dumb hillbilly. He pinched his lips together instead.

Obie examined the black hole, the night outside. He had cause to be afraid. If Bas, and Virg, too, had seen the burying mound, felt the hate coming from its heart, been pulled into the river, then sucked down into the cave of the giant pigtoe . . . Obie's mind rattled on. At first he found satisfaction in every thought, agreed with them all until he began to listen. Soon the excuses sounded all too familiar and Obie thought about his daddy, of all the people and events he blamed for his misfortunes. Obie swallowed hard. Was he doing the same? Obie didn't believe he was yellow. Maybe what ran down his back was a streak of Dalton Wilks. The realization failed to help Obie set aside the crippling fear that squeezed his heart.

A jarring clap of thunder shook the night; cracks of white light broke inside the sky, allowing Obie time to search for the Immortals and the fear their forms invoked.

"I ain't telling you again." Bas reached down, took a handful of suspender and pulled Obie to his feet. "I'm fixing to leave and we're going together. If you want me to knock you up side the head and tote you, I will."

Bas's doubled fist rose between them—a big, bony fist with huge, flat knuckles. Bas owned a reputation that Obie always thought an exaggeration but the flattened knuckles, the muscles in the forearm, changed his mind. Obie raised his hand to the fist. "You won't have to tote me and you won't have to knock me silly."

Obie slid his feet into soggy shoes, wrapped the laces around his ankles several times before knotting them. Somehow he knew Bas was right about getting across the Sallapoosa but crossing it in the dark filled Obie with another terror. Finding the pearls seemed the easy part now; getting them home was the pie-in-the-sky part of his plan.

The Nun Yuna Wi existed; he knew it, knew they would keep after him until they had their pearls. Obie turned his back on Bas, on the cave's opening. He stepped ahead a half step, pretending to look for the tow sack. The search took no longer than a single moment, but in that instant of time, Obie's only thought was, *God, I don't know what this is all about, just help me to get back home with my pearls.*

"My tow sack," he said, pretending impatience, "I can't—"

"It's here in my hand." Bas threw it as Obie turned. "I don't know what's eating on you but you best bury it in your hip pocket until we get ourselves across that river. If you fall in, I ain't jumping in to save you. Chaser," Bas called out, "get yourself up here. Don't want to be fretting over you neither."

"You won't have to be worrying about me." Obie reached down and retrieved the packet of pearls. He squeezed it inside his hand before pushing it to the bottom of his pocket, then he stepped past Bas and the smoking embers of their fire.

Obie chose not to pause once he left the safety of the cave. He sidestepped his way along the ledge and past the spring. He climbed over boulders, through bushes, and hugged the sheer vertical wall that took him down toward that ribbon of ground that dipped in the center. Obie thought about the Immortals each time he took a step or drew in a breath but the terrain, the dark and threatening storm, demanded all of his attention. "Chaser," he shouted, "get back here where I can see you."

Wind whipped against his face, whistled in his ears. It slashed at the vines and unleashed the odors of witch hazel and sorrel. Lightning, in its momentary flashes, revealed the descending slope and the parallel walls of vegetation.

"Hold up, Obie." Bas moved off the trail and stepped aside a few steps. He paused there long enough to draw his fingers across the bark of a chestnut. When lightning struck again, Obie saw the deep slash mark. "We're headed just right," Bas yelled, and moved back to Obie's side. "Since it's me that knows the way, I'll take the lead. You want to tote my turkey?"

Obie shook his head and Bas added, "I ain't much for singing; sound just like a jackass with a bellyache. But when you stop hearing my cackle, you take to yelling. And Chaser," he said, "you stay close. Got no time to go looking for you."

Bas reached back and gave Obie's shoulder a shake. "You hear what I told you?"

"I heard."

"I ain't crazy, Obie. And you're gonna have to trust me same as I trusted you to get us here."

Bas whirled around. His deep, raspy voice lent itself to the howling wind. Obie took two steps for each of Bas's. He lifted his legs high to avoid tripping and kept his eyes glued on the back of Chaser's head. Though Bas was right about his singing, it took on a compelling sound as the storm grew closer and the forest closed around them.

Obie refused to look right or left, felt as if he were walking with his eyes shut. He concentrated on lifting his knees, feeling his weight roll onto the ball of one foot, then the other. Had he grown accustomed to crawling through the impossible thickets of dog-hobble and spice-bush, the nearly impenetrable tangles of wild grape and serviceberry, the prickly and stinging switches that lashed across his face? Was it the approaching storm that hurried him along and made the intolerable tolerable? Was it the liquid air and the promise of a downpour? Or was it the faceless forms from the depths of the sucking pot, which worked their way into Obie's mind, that made his heart pound against his chest, lengthen his stride, count numbers to occupy his thoughts on something other than the Nun Yuna Wi? All of it, he reasoned, as the mysterious silence of the high valley and burying mound picked at his brain until finally breaking through the flood of numbers. "Wait!" he yelled and ran to catch up.

Had the sucking pot really opened and taken him into the world of the Immortals? Were those stories he remembered from childhood really true? Had his life been spared for a special reason?

Obie wanted to disregard his full belly, the sweet sticky taste of honey on his lips. He tried to focus on the cut above his ear, the knot on the side of his head, the bruises over his body. He tried to convince himself that it was the battering his body took in the river. The river was to blame for the strange confusion swirling inside his head.

Lightning cut across the sky. Thunder ripped in behind each brilliant flash. More lightning and shadows from every direction reeled through the forest. He saw figures, heard them whispering. He tried to move faster but his legs refused. It was as dark as the devil's pocket, Obie thought, and he strained to see through the blackness. "Bas," Obie shouted, "wait up. You're getting too far ahead."

"Ain't much farther." Bas waited, his rifle resting on his shoulder and Chaser beside him. "We can rest a spell if you need to catch up to your breath."

Obie shook his head. He reached down to grab hold of Chaser. "Just don't go so fast," he said. "I'm tired as a cur dog dragging a string of tin cans."

Each step became a tortured effort. It took Obie closer to the river and the inevitable crossing. Lightning flashed; the mist grew heavier. Soon it turned to rain. Obie wiped the moisture from his eyes. It soaked his hair to his head and dripped down his neck to run the length of his spine while the constant buffeting of wind chilled him through. It was stupid being out on such a night, stupid to think they could successfully cross the river in the dark. "Stupid, dumb hillbilly," Obie shouted, his anger propelling him through the forest to that place they had crossed the Sallapoosa days earlier.

"Now that we're here," Obie shouted, "look out there. Can't see a blessed thing. Just how are we gonna cross it?"

"I told you to trust me; I got it all figured," Bas responded.

Bas's calm irritated Obie, who jerked free of the big hand that clutched his arm. Yet he continued to follow Bas. They stopped several feet back from the river's edge. Between flashes of lightning, Obie saw water splashing wildly against the graybacks. "Next time there's a flash, you look out over that water for as far as you can see. Near as I can recollect, the things we used to cross on were a good foot out of the water." Bas pointed down at the shallows. "Can't tell for certain how far the river's come up but it 'pears to be a foot or more."

"You said you had an idea for getting across. It better be a good one or I'm staying right here until daylight."

"You stay here until daylight and you'll be standing in the river. That bank ain't gonna hold diddly-squat. River's gonna fill up this whole bottom." Bas pulled his hat down onto his ears. "Our only chance is to get across before the real storm hits. It's a-coming, too. If you listen close, you can hear it a-rumbling far off."

Bas stepped back. "We ain't toting nothing extra neither."

Booming volleys of thunder rang in Obie's ears. Lightning transformed the forest into a spooky graveyard of ghostly shadows and set the sky aflame with incendiary webs of silver-gray threads. Giant trees exploded and filled the air with the scent of their flaming demise. Rain began. It hit Obie's head, then came in a rush.

"I told you we was gonna get it!" Bas thrust a three-foot length of green sumac into Obie's hand. "Nearest thing you got to being dry is your shirt," he said. "Take it off."

"Take it off? It's cold."

"Just do it!" Bas shouted. "Got no time to bicker."

"This is my best shirt."

Bas thrust a knife at Obie. "You want I should cut it off?"

Obie unwillingly removed his coat, dropped his suspenders, unbuttoned his best shirt. Rain stung his bare back. "Hold it out," Bas yelled, then pressed a ball of sticky pine pitch into the center of the cloth. "Rub it in good and if you got extra socks or such, roll them all together. The bigger wick you can make the longer the torch will burn."

"Where did you get the pitch?"

"Found it up in that high valley this morning. Figured we'd be a-needing it for starting fires. How you think I got that one in the cave going so quick?"

Obie recalled smelling the pitch; he had smelled it at the mound, too, and at the bottom of the sucking pot. Obie blinked away the rain, reasoning that if he smelled it when he thought he was at the bottom of the sucking pot, then all of his terrible memories were due to a knock on the head. The Nun Yuna Wi were just a part of being unconscious . . . weren't they?

Obie rubbed pitch into two pairs of socks, into his best shirt, too. He wrapped them tightly about the stick and secured the knot of cloth with thin wire from his tow sack. "Where did you learn how to do this?"

"My daddy learned me."

"What about Chaser? How's she gonna get across?"

"Same way she got to this side." Bas emptied his tow sack before slitting it with his knife, then rolled it into a long sling, attached it to his rifle to carry across his back. He stuffed the bag of shells and his quilt behind the bib of his overalls. "Let's head out. Ain't gonna get none better."

Obie twisted the button on the pocket of his overalls. *Help me to get these pearls home.* He pressed his palm flat against the pocket until feeling the thump of his heart. *Help me to get these pearls home.* Obie stuffed his quilt behind the bib of his overalls. He started to put on his coat, felt the weight of the soggy wool fabric and reconsidered. If he fell in . . . if he fell in, it wouldn't matter a whole terrible lot what he was wearing and Obie left it behind with his tow sack, its contents and the turkey. "Chaser, come over here."

"Soon as I get that thing fired up, you get." Bas struck a match. "Got no idea how long it'll burn, so keep moving."

As they started toward the river, Bas lit his torch from Obie's. "Can you remember where we crossed before?" Obie asked.

But Bas failed to respond and Obie tried to remember . . . boulders big as bears on the far side, broken logs, deadfall, tree stumps, their spiderlike roots catching bits of hide and moss, all of it a jumbled trap on the river's deep and churning outside curve.

"Get a-going," Bas shouted, and gave Obie a push toward the litter of chipped rock and gravel beneath the river's shallow side. "Get out there you dang dog."

Water swirled around Obie's ankles. It splashed against his knees. He raised the torch higher for a view longer than his next step. But wind whipped the flame in the opposite direction. Rain hissed against it and pelted his face. Before he reached the submerged gravel bar, Obie felt the pull of the current against his knees. Panic reached up to paralyze his mind. He tried to ignore the still-too-fresh memory of the sucking pot, the strangling sensation that had seemed to squeeze his brain flat. "Chaser," Obie shouted, "you better be behind me. Mamma will have my hide if I lose you." And Obie's voice wavered with the wind.

Arms of a gnarled stump and tips of its roots reached up from the swirling water. He needed to be careful, surefooted. He aimed his torch at the water, at the next step. But the rain fell faster now. It hit his face, his bare hide like pellets of rock salt. It blurred his vision. Each time he blinked the distortions away, he lost focus and teetered on one foot unsurely.

"Dang it, Obie, get a move on; these torches ain't gonna last."

Obie closed his eyes. *Help me to get these pearls home.* He climbed over the stump and through its dead roots. He used the gnarled arm as a springboard and leaped toward a jumble of dead trees that thrashed precariously in the current. Fear stiffened his legs. It dulled his mind. *Help me to get these pearls home.* Thinking the words pushed the crippling affliction aside. It allowed him to refocus all of his attention on the swaying shadows hiding beneath the water's surface. He concentrated on lifting one leg at a time, shifting his balance, trusting the log to support his weight that needed split second before leaping ahead the next step. And each time, Obie grabbed through the darkness for something to hold.

He knew better than to stop. If he hesitated a moment fear would master him; it would freeze him to the spot and make him its victim. He paused only long enough to catch his balance, then plan the next step.

A partially submerged tree stretched out into the dark and rose at an angle above the river's surface. If he remembered correctly the stump rested inside a jumble of graybacks. Instead of walking heel-to-toe, Obie dropped onto his bottom. Water reached up to his belly. It pulled at him as he scooted ahead.

Wind, a constant drone now, drove rain, dried leaves and twigs through the air. Lightning and thunder continued to bounce across the valley while a distant roar flowed with the river. Obie heard it. From the east, he thought, and started to look up. But in the split second it took to decide, Obie felt a cold shiver; his mind shrieked. He yelled. He locked his feet beneath the log as he felt himself slip.

"Move it," Bas shouted.

Obie sucked in the cold air. He squeezed his hands and tensed his muscles to stop their quivering before he started ahead. Rain battered his face. Thunder whirled inside the wind. Lightning burst across the sky, revealing graybacks just ahead.

Water crashed against them. It churned and whirled in a circular motion. Did a sucking pot hide beneath the dark surface? Obie bit his lower lip. He loosened his hold on the log, drew one leg up and planted his knee. To keep from being swept away, Obie leaned against the current. He pushed with the same force it pushed against him. He drew his other knee up. Cautiously he crawled ahead until the graybacks were within reach. He warned himself about rising too quickly, about planting his foot too solidly on the slick surface.

Help me to get these pearls home. Obie dragged one leg behind the other. He shifted the torch to the right hand so he could reach out with the left. Slowly he leaned forward. His body bent in the middle until the tips of his fingers touched the slick mossy surface. And Obie made a final lunge. "You back there?"

If Bas responded, his reply lost itself in the thunder. Obie wanted to look around, to satisfy his mind that Chaser was there and Bas behind her. Terror grasped his heart and rose into his throat like vomit. He tried to swallow, but his torch flickered and a new panic yanked him to his feet. It thrust him over one grayback, then another until he reached the last one.

Days ago, he had made the leap from land to rock in one long stride. Of course he had the advantage of a running start that day, a fresh body, a sense of excitement that fear and fatigue now stole. And the river had risen, three feet at least. It rushed over his ankles and flowed above the bank. Obie, in an effort to see how far it extended, raised his torch toward the deep, outside curve. It flickered badly. He considered waiting, letting Bas go first. Bas was taller; he had a longer reach, was stronger, too. It would be an easy leap for someone with long legs. And Bas had bigger hands. All Obie thought about was having Bas on the bank when he jumped, so if he fell short . . .

But Bas couldn't swim. The thought rattled inside Obie's brain. He squeezed his eyes shut. *Help me to get these pearls home.*

He knew he wouldn't make it. He jumped. He yelled. The torch fell from his hand. Instead of hitting feet first, being thrown backward, Obie stretched ahead, his arms reaching, his fingers clawing. He grabbed for the beargrass he remembered growing on the bank. Water flowed over it now. His hands opened and closed . . . beargrass, switch cane, tree root, anything!

"Hang on," Bas yelled. "I'm a-coming."

Bas's big hand grabbed Obie by the shoulder straps, pulled him from the current. "Thought I was a goner," Obie sputtered while spitting up mouthfuls of muddy water. "Where's Chaser? She didn't make it, did she? She got swept away, I know it."

As Bas pulled Obie through knee-deep water, he

said, "You run on, Obie, like an old man with ants up his pants. It's no wonder Virg shuts his ears to you."

Before Obie crawled free of the mud and water, he felt Chaser's warm tongue on the side of his face. He rolled over onto his back, put both arms around her, buried his face against her wet fur.

But Bas yanked on his suspenders. "Stop wooling that dog and let's get. There's a wall of water coming out of them hills what'll flood this whole bottom. It's been rumbling like a locomotive ever since we started across."

"You remember those caves up along that limestone ledge?" Obie asked. "We can stay in one of them until the storm lets up."

"Sounds good but I'm taking the lead. With me breaking the way it'll be a whole lot faster." Bas's voice came out of his throat like a handful of gravel. "Ain't because I want a varmint to get you neither. Any varmint with good sense has got to high ground."

"Bas," Obie's voice faltered, "you were right about getting across the river. And maybe Virg is right about me being an aggravation. I'm sorry."

"Dang it, Obie, I told you we got no time for sappy stuff like that."

A deep peal of thunder rolled off the ridge top, then sank into the sodden bottom. Obie pulled his quilt from behind the bib of his overalls and threw it over his shoulders. He turned back to look at the river and the wilderness. Like his great-granddaddy Wilks, he, too, had gone to River Country and lived to tell about it. "Come on, Chaser. Once we cross the big river, it's a straight shot home."

CHAPTER

12

* * *

OBIE RAISED HIS FACE TO THE SKY, OPENED HIS MOUTH AND felt the cool rain trickle down his parched throat. He could not recall such a storm or hearing his kinfolk talk about one lasting so long. It moved across the sky, northeast, like it was done with them, then it swung around and passed overhead, rumbling and carrying on worse than the time before. It banged off the limestone walls, the ledges that jutted out above the valley, cracked the sky wide open. Rain filled his pores, saturated his lungs and rang inside his brain. It kept on and on until he wanted to yell, smash something. There was no way of escaping it, no place to hide.

"This here is the by-damnedest storm I ever seen," Bas yelled.

Obie tried to keep pace with Bas up the rocky and steeply sloping hillside. But he tired quickly and fell farther behind. Saplings reached above his shoulders. Wild grape and saw briars pricked his bare arms and face, tripped him and sent him stumbling ahead. Each few steps were miles long and rung from him every bit of his remaining strength. His muscles heaved in spasms of hot and cold. He wondered if he would ever be warm again.

Volleys of thunder, lightning crackling like live electrical wires, followed him toward the ridge. If the storm continued, he knew they would have trouble getting home; might even be a race to get there before the first of the month. Wet wind hissed and wailed down through the pines. Several times Obie stopped to adjust the quilt across his shoulders, to listen and reassure himself that it was only wind following him to the ledge. To occupy his thoughts, Obie filled his mind with home: sleeping in his bed, his mamma's cooking, dry clothes, warm fire, he even considered Virg's reaction to the pearls.

"It ain't far now," Bas called back.

The ledge jutted out above them. Obie saw its long, dark shadow during the brief flashes. Seeing it, knowing it was finally within reach, encouraged him to continue the slow, arduous climb, though it was with stiff legs now, as his gait turned into a painful limp.

Obie's feet burned. The wet shoes hardened and chafed his heels, rubbing them until each time he took another step, warm blood seeped beneath his heel and into the hollow below the arch.

"Over here," Bas shouted. "I found it. Obie? Obie, where in tarnation are you?"

Chaser's bark brought him to Obie's side. "Don't look like you got much snap left," Bas said and reached out to help.

When Obie jerked away from Bas's outstretched

hand, Bas caught hold of Obie's arm and drew it over his shoulder. "Ain't knowd a Wilks yet that weren't stubborn as a taproot, but you're the worst."

Bas supported Obie's weight the last hundred yards. "This here cave is better than the others; got a shelf over the opening, and there's near-dry brush for a fire."

Years of wind and rain had carved a broad hollow in the layers. Bas sent Chaser into the dark hole first, waiting a minute before crouching down and dragging Obie behind. "This here place don't smell too awful good. Ain't much deeper than I am long neither." He propped Obie against the wall. "Feels good to be outta that rain; feel a whole lot better with a fire."

Obie trembled. His eyes dropped shut, yet the ringing inside his head continued. Besides being cold and wet, he was caught inside a limp and useless body, trapped and helpless to save himself from the heavy thickening that washed through his mind, that seeped down into every part of his being, leaving him easy prey for whatever lurked nearby.

"Obie, is that you? Your teeth is a-rattling just like a hog eating charcoal."

But Obie had already closed his eyes upon Bas's fire. And from the dark, howling night rose the featureless faces of the Nun Yuna Wi to hover just outside the cave's opening, to stare at him through hollow eyes. Obie jerked straight. He stared back, blinked to refocus upon the empty opening. "Chaser," Obie called, "come here, girl."

Obie spread his legs, pushed Chaser down between them. He drew her back on her haunches until her shoulders pressed against the packet of pearls. She stunk, stunk bad, but in a few moments her warmth spread through him, and he rested his head against her. His eyelids fell shut. He drifted off, further and further, until he slipped beyond the point of half sleep.

Fog settled the length of the hollow and slithered up the curve of the ridge side. It softened the gullied land, the fresh reddish scars that bled down the northerly slope. It thickened in low-lying places, hung greenish over pasture lands and brownish above the corn. It hid the trickle of spring water, bubbling out from the rocky hillside, then falling off into the sink. Not a sound escaped it. It outlined the house, the sideling south side and sloping porch. It obscured moss growing between the plank flooring, concealed the empty rocker, held together now with nails and baling wire. A garden spot and barns waited, too, in the hazed-over distance. South of the large barn a rail fence grew up from the black earth. Mattie Mae Wilks's mule slept behind eight-foot lengths of old chestnut, mended now with strands of barbed wire, pine and scrub brush scuffed off into the decaying corners. At first glance, fog appeared to fill the entire enclosure but a closer look revealed something glistening white in the center of the pen.

Fog ringed the wobbly circle. It framed shafts of sunlight that fell down from a blue sky to warm the air and shimmer like waves of a distant mirage. And, too, it hid the identities of those who stood among the shadows and looked in. Soon though, a breeze stirred. Besides mixing the air and all of its scents, wind thinned the fog and revealed the faces of those who waited outside the pen. Obie stood on one side; the Immortals on his right; Mattie Mae Wilks and her children on his left. Instead of observing one another, they focused their attention upon a pastel iridescence that filled the emptiness and surrounded a pair of glistening white shoes.

Obie admired the white leather shoes and their pearl

laces. He took pleasure in watching them and that pleasure drew him closer until his belly crowded the rail. He raised his hands to the old wood. Its unevenness pressed against his palms while sunlight warmed his skin and made him comfortable all over.

The fog, which cast high walls about the circular clearing, confined the sun's rays and laid down a carpet of pinks and lavender, blues and green. It melted them into fused rivulets of iridescence that shimmered on the toes of the white shoes.

The shoes sashayed from one end of the pen to the other, one side to the opposite side. They twirled on their toes, and clicked their heels; they feinted one way, then spun around and glided the other; they danced a jig and tapped their toes. They whirled in circles, played and teased over every inch of the railed enclosure.

Obie's admiration of the shoes flourished, but soon he tired of just watching. He wanted to try on the shoes, learn to dance the same way they danced. He felt desire swell inside his chest. It made him smile and shuffle his feet to a rhythm he had never before heard. He raised his leg to crawl between the rails but rusty barbed wire, used to hold the old chestnut logs together, kept him from inside the pen. Obie started right but the Immortals were there. He turned left but his mamma and her children filled that space. Obie moved back to his place at the fence. He crouched down and eased his arm between strands of wire until he reached inside the circle where the white shoes continued to dance.

They side-stepped up the center, twirled in wide sweeping circles, jumped up or hopped back when Obie's hand came too close. Always the shoes were quicker than his fingers. He felt ridiculous being unable to catch the shoes. He was sure *that those watching him thought it laughable, too. But the Immortals remained hidden inside their empty faces and glowing bodies while his mamma looked more angry than amused.*

Determined now, Obie raised his foot to the first rail. He climbed, ladder-fashion, until he swung his leg over the top length of chestnut. But the knee of his overalls caught on the rusty wire. Instead of jerking and tearing free, then dropping headlong into the pen, Obie's upbringing made him consider; the overalls had been bought for Virg; Orvull wore them a short time; now they were his; before Christmas they would pass on to Josh; they needed to be more than patches on patches. Obie twisted right, left, moved his hips up and down, wrenched his shoulders back and forth. But the barb refused to release the knee of his overalls. He cursed the hook, his inner fiber that made him considerate of Josh. He called to his mamma for help, to the Immortals who had spared him for some special purpose, but none budged from their places.

It occured to Obie to let go, fall back to the ground and content himself with observing the shoes. But he wanted to wear them. He wanted to walk inside them, feel their soft texture. He wanted to dance and go where they would lead him, so Obie continued to struggle.

He struggled throughout the night with the barbed wire. He thrashed his legs, rolled one way, then the other until finally opening his eyes.

A suspicion of light crept over the eastern ridge while a thick vaporous haze filled the valley and reached over the ledge. It seeped into the cave. Obie shivered. A crawling hunger wiggled inside his empty belly. He added bits of dry twigs, needles and leaves to the bed of coals, then sat back and thought about the white shoes, their strings of pearl laces. Why had the shoes been so elusive and he so bumble-fingered? What did the dream mean? Obie chewed on the inside of his cheek while many thoughts pushed at his mind.

The big river lay a full day's walk to the north. So much rain would require extra time to skirt the low places. Unless they reached Torrey's landing with enough daylight for the crossing, that old man would make them wait until morning. Leaving the cave, and leaving it soon, struck Obie as being the most important of his thoughts. "Bas, wake up," he said, urgency tainting his tone. "Time we was putting this wilderness behind us."

CHAPTER
13

∗ ∗ ∗

BEFORE THEY LEFT THE CAVE, THEY DEBATED THE ADVAN-
tages of heading west to Scaggs Ford or east to Hunters
Town, rather than paying Bub Torrey with pearls to take
them across the big river. But to go west or east would
take them miles out of their way. "And the chances of our
catching a ride real quick," Obie said, "might be slim to
nothing."

Bas raised his rifle to his shoulder. "I ain't got a warm
spot on me, my quilt ain't worth the carrying home, my
belly's wrinkled as last year's apples, but I'm grateful it
ain't raining."

They left their soggy quilts behind and headed north
into a foggy morning. Dim outlines surrounded them.
Everything dripped, soggy to walk upon, while pale light
lay in streaks above the treetops. The damp cold worked
its way through the still-wet fibers of Obie's overalls. He
wished for the coat he had left on the other side of the

Sallapoosa but consoled himself with thoughts of home
. . . sitting at the kitchen table with his back to the stove
and talking to his mamma. He would have to tell her of
his decision to go north. He would tell her that his going
would be good for the family; he would send money
regularly. Mattie Mae Wilks was good with a dollar; it
was his daddy who had holes in his pockets. But for all
of the reasoning, and no matter how right it all sounded,
Obie knew his mamma would not take kindly to his
leaving. She'd be madder than a rooster in an empty hen
house.

Obie watched Chaser trot ahead. He would miss his
dog, miss Josh, his sisters, too. But he would come home
often, more often than Uncle Tully came home. He
would buy Josh and Caleb fishing poles, teach them to
catch the big ones; he would tell Delsie and Orrie about
things in the city; he would bring home jellied orange
slices and baby dolls for Selena and Loranda. Going north
would be good for the whole Wilks family. God's will,
Obie told himself.

His mamma always said, *"The good Lord don't do no
explaining but He lets a-body know what He wants. An' if
that body shuts his mind to the Lord's way, that body's life
is sure to turn to sixes and sevens."*

Things were going too well to suspect that they
would suddenly turn to sixes and sevens. Finding the
pearls, being spared by the Immortals, paying off Arvis
Cagley, then going north was all part of God's will. Obie
knew it and yelled, "Mamma's sure to see the light!"

The slope of the ground angled downward and took
them inside a deciduous forest with all of its thickets and
briars crowding for space. Signs of the storm's ferocity

lay everywhere: trees split in half, limbs, thicker than a man's arm, broken, mud slides and gaping gullies, scrub uprooted. "Hey," Obie called out, "you have any idea what day it is or what time of the month?"

"Nope, but I can tell you that my belly wishes it had that turkey we went and left on the other side of the Sallapoosa."

"Any chance of Chaser scaring up something?"

"Ain't likely. Only thing that dog wants is to crawl under a cabin and sleep." Bas glanced back. "Only hope we got of eating is to find a honey tree. I been a-looking but I can't see for all this fog."

They fell quiet and moved on in a silence that reached out in every direction. The usual murmur of sound and motion, no more discernible than a breeze, was missing. But captured inside the gray fog were pungent and earthy odors that made the air oppressive.

As the steep descent leveled off to rolling and irregular terrain, water filled the low areas, rivulets exposed roots and washed hollows from beneath graybacks. The ground was a mire and slowed their pace as they kept a northward direction.

They skirted submerged thickets and other watery places where dead bodies of skunk and 'possum floated on murky water. Bas cautioned Obie about snakes and other poisonous creatures that lurked along the shallow edges. "Every bottom that we have to cross is gonna be just like that a-one," he said as they began the ascent toward the next dividing ridge.

The cloudy and soggy day dragged along, one tedious step after another. By midday they came on remnants of the old bridge spanning Morney Creek. Support timbers and splinters of the hand-hewn planks were all that remained. The creek ran well over its banks, knee to waist high in low places. "If I never see another creek it'll be too soon," Bas said and started across.

Chaser went second, Obie followed. It took an hour longer than normal to cross the hollow. But when they reached the ridge above Gullet Valley, Bas said, "Lawdy, lawdy, will you lookie down there."

"It's a lake!" Obie blew out his lips. "You see any way to cross to the other side?"

"Going around makes a whole lot more sense."

Obie rolled his head back. Tiny patches of blue showed through the continually thinning layers of gray. "That's two, maybe three miles," Obie said. "If I remember rightly, it's an hour's walk from the other side of this valley to the big river."

"To make it before dark," Bas said, "we'll have to hop-skip a-ways."

"I feel as if I've hop-skipped the whole day."

Bas grinned. "It's them wee-short legs you got."

Obie's lips pinched tight together before he realized Bas was teasing.

"How come you to be so touchy over what you can't help?" Bas asked. "Being a feist ain't no sin; it's being a feist that makes a racket, then hides when trouble starts. You ain't that sort."

Obie flicked his wrists, impatient, embarrassed by Bas's compliment. "You think Mr. Torrey will let us stay the night in his barn and give us some supper?"

"For a share of them pearls, that old buzzard'll give us his whole place." Bas slid his hat back onto his forehead. "How far you judge Iversol to be? You remember the smell in that general store? It were like going to a candy pie supper. Just thinking on it gives me a belly-ache."

Obie remembered: open barrels of beans, sugar and flour; fresh-ground coffee; tanned hides stacked in the back; tobacco plugs; spices; bolts of cloth that smelled like his mamma's fresh-washed dress; pine tar soap; jars of jaw-breakers, horehound candy, jellied orange slices, licorice, strawberry soda, Moon Pies. Better than any candy pie supper he could remember.

The remembering twisted Obie's belly into knots. "If our luck holds, we'll pick up a ride right off tomorrow; might be someone going all the way to the junction."

They stood together, Chaser sitting in front of them, each locked into his own thoughts. But Chaser's bark snapped them back to the moment. "Ain't gonna get home standing here," Bas said and started west.

Gullet Valley was a combination of forest, logging area, and cultivated land. They circled the west end before cutting north and angling toward the crest of the next ridge. Bas pointed down into the fog-shrouded bottom before they began the steep descent at a half run. He ignored the thickets, circling some, crashing through others. He jumped fallen trees and used graybacks as springboards. At the bottom, he paused, but only long enough for Obie to catch up. "If we follow the bottom around, it's an extra two miles. If we don't, we gotta climb that-there hill and cross over the ridge. You got enough snap left in you?"

Obie shook off the notion of going around. Without responding, he stepped ahead and started the steep climb through the gray haze. He had no idea about the exact number of miles that separated him from home but the knowledge of being so close put a bounce back into his step, made him forget the blisters on his heels, the gnawing inside his middle.

As afternoon passed and the sun dropped in the west, the overhead clouds pushed eastward, leaving behind a brilliantly clear sky. Trees wore fresh green while sunlight burned off the oppressive odors of earth and decay. Fingers of light reached through the canopy of trees, leaving lacy shadows across their path.

Chaser perked her ears just before Obie yelled, "It's down there. I can hear it."

"Dang fog," Bas sputtered. "It's gonna be dark 'fore we get down there."

"No, sir," Obie shouted and started to run. "Can you make out where the Torrey place is?"

"Not yet."

They raced through an area of timbered land, a stand of dying chestnut trees. They ran until fog closed around them. It obscured the sun, left them to weave their way through thickets of sumac, yellow root and saw briar, which claimed the wet ground along the lower elevation. Obie kept his head cocked to the left, as if listening for instructions that would take him to that place on the river opposite Bub Torrey's cabin.

As they moved closer the sound of the river became an uninterrupted drone and they waded the treacherous overflow to find the original bank. "That cable line has to be nearby." Obie shouted. "I smell smoke."

"Over there!"

"I see it! Cabin's right beneath it. You see it?"

Bas unshouldered the rifle. He slid a shell into the

chamber, fired. "Bet that old coot got more than his feet wet when this river went."

"He's got to be there." Obie spun around to look at Bas. "Fire again. Why would smoke be coming out of that chimney if he isn't there?"

Bas reloaded the rifle, fired a second shot. They waited. They watched. "It's over a half day's walk if we have to go by way of Scaggs Ford. Fire again, Bas."

"It don't look like Mr. Torrey's to home. Might be that he's off in Iversol on a toot."

"He has to be there. We need to be across this river."

They waited. Was Bub Torrey off on a toot? Bas fired twice more before someone stepped from the cabin and started down toward the river.

"It's him!" Obie gave Bas's shoulder a punch. "He's coming for us."

They watched him wade the water to reach his flat-bottomed ferry and connect the pulley line to the cable. Obie closed his eyes. *Thank you for helping me get my pearls home.*

"We have to get out there, Bas, where he can pick us up. Come on, Chaser." Obie started ahead. Water crept above his knees. He guessed that it might rise over his head before he reached the cable station, and there was sure to be a strong current. Obie stopped . . . Bas couldn't swim!

They had to get out to the end of Bub Torrey's cable. "Bas," Obie said, "you're gonna have to trust me."

Bas raised a bushy blond eyebrow and Obie guessed that Bas was thinking about their crossing the Sallapoosa and his less than courageous attitude. "I'm a real strong swimmer, Bas, and if you'll just relax I know I can get us out to the end of that cable."

Bas considered the river, the unknown depth and the end of the cable. "Whatcha want I should do?"

"The strongest current will be between the river banks but there will likely be some pull before we get out that far." Obie felt the packet safe inside his overall pocket. "I know that getting your rifle wet won't be good for it but you have to let me carry it over my back with that sling you made."

Obie waded out until the water reached his waist. "Don't be scared," he said. "And when I tell you to stretch out and kick, don't fight me."

Bas took the rifle from over his shoulder and handed it to Obie. His Adam's apple bobbed up and down and his cheeks went pale. "You don't want to sleep out another night, do you?" Obie asked. "And isn't your belly just as empty as mine?"

Bas studied Obie silently while he eyed the rise of the water, the pull against his body. Finally he waded out farther while Chaser swam alongside.

"Soon as your feet don't touch, you roll over onto your back," Obie instructed. "And whatever you do, don't pull on me."

Obie paddled ahead. The depth of the water rose past Bas's suspenders, then rose to his shoulders. When it reached his chin, he jerked back. "You're okay," Obie shouted. "Lay easy."

Obie pulled himself through the water. "Relax, Bas! Don't fight me or you'll sink us both."

"Obie!" Bas yelled.

"Kick your feet!"

Obie swam dog fashion, using his legs to push ahead and one arm to pull himself toward the flat-bottomed boat. Bub Torrey waved him over. "You're doing fine, youngster. Keep a-coming."

Chaser was already on board and shaking herself while Obie struggled against the current and the dead weight stretching out his arm. "It's okay, Bas. Hang on." Obie spit out the muddy water that splashed in his face. "We're almost there. Another ten feet."

"Hurry!" A quiver rattled through Bas's voice. "Hurry."

"Think on fried chicken, Bas, some grits and gravy, hot biscuits to push it down."

"I'm a-thinking, Obie. I'm a-thinking."

The closer he swam toward the boat the stronger the current. If he missed catching hold of the cable, he and Bas would likely be carried halfway across the state before escaping the river. "Throw me a line, mister. Throw it quick."

"I'm a-sinking, Obie."

"No you're not! Throw me a line," Obie screamed to the ferryman. "Hurry, throw me a line."

The rope splashed in front of him and Obie grabbed it. "I got it, Bas. We're gonna be okay. I got the line."

"Pull us in, mister."

Obie's arms felt as if they were being yanked from their sockets. When he reached up and caught the side of the boat, he said, "Get my friend out first." And he pulled Bas ahead so that he could reach up and grip the cable with one hand, Bub Torrey's arm with the other.

Obie pushed on Bas's rump until Bas threw a leg over the side of the boat, then Obie grabbed for the cable and pulled himself out of the water.

"Damn," Bas said, "you're a helluva swimmer." Bas came close to hugging Obie but caught himself and added, "How'd you ever learn to swim so good?"

"Virg taught me," Obie said. "He used to think it was great fun throwing me in the creek. He stopped when I learned to swim."

Bub Torrey turned the pulley in the opposite direction. "You two can give me a hand here."

Chaser disliked the boat; she cried all the way across. Obie understood her fright and held her around the body so she wouldn't jump out. The muddy water bucked and washed across their feet. Dead fall and tree limbs crashed against the boat, lifting it out of the water, tipping it. But the cable brought it back.

By the time they reached Bub Torrey's landing, Bas looked more blue than tan. Chaser leaped out first, swam for high ground. Bas took his rifle and followed Chaser up the hill while Obie helped Bub Torrey tie down his boat. "Sure didn't figure on ever seeing the two of you again."

"Must have been some kind of storm that ripped through here."

"Worst I ever seen. Everything went plumb to hell, lickety-split. You two ever get to Fraser's Crossing?"

Fraser's Crossing? Obie recalled his lie. "No, sir, we sure didn't. When the storm hit we decided against visiting my kinfolk, decided it was wisdom to turn back. Sure do appreciate your coming across to pick us up."

"You got my four bits, ain't you?"

"Yes, sir, I can pay." Obie jumped from the boat, waded the water to high ground. "Can you tell me the day, Mr. Torrey, and the date?"

"It's Wednesday. The twenty-eighth, I do believe, but I got a calendar inside."

Bub Torrey was a round-faced man, a head taller than Obie. He wore overalls, a floppy brimmed felt hat, blue shirt with patched elbows and high-top shoes. Obie doubted that Bub was as old as his granddaddy but old enough to have lost all of his teeth. He chewed tobacco, shaved only when it pleased him, and smelled as if he disliked washing, too. He invited the boys inside.

"Bring your dog," he said. "What's its name?"

"Chaser," Obie replied. "Best dog there is."

"Had me a cat dog years back." Rusty hinges squeaked as he threw open the door. "That dog'd run a cat to death before he'd let up. Never seen another like him."

The cabin felt warm and was lit by a lantern. The logs bore the axe marks of being hand-cut but the seams between them had never been chinked. A continual draft caused the lantern to flicker and cast wiggly shadows on the overhead beams and open loft. A narrow ladder leaned against the fieldstone fireplace. Obie's gaze followed the rungs to the loft, then fixed itself on a pair of shiny rat eyes that peered down at him. Obie's skin rippled.

"Nope," Bub Torrey took the calendar from a nail, "it's Thursday the twenty-ninth. I know that's right because I went to Iversol day before yesterday and that were Tuesday. Had to get me some kerosene. Dang flood stole my barrel, took it clean down the river."

"Sir"—Obie backed up to the stove's warmth—"my name's Obadiah Wilks and my friend is Bas Allardice. I'd like to—"

"Allardice you say?" He pursed his lips before he asked, "You kin to Sarson?"

"He's my daddy," Bas replied. "You know him?"

"Know of him." Bub smacked his lips. "Shore wish I had me a jug, just for keeping the chill from my joints, you understand." Bub turned to Obie. "You got my four bits?"

"We don't mean to be a botherment to you, Mr. Torrey, but we were wondering if we could pay extra for supper and staying the night. We'll be gone come sunup."

Bub scratched beneath the front of his battered hat. "Can you eat stew?"

"You bet!"

"Then get out of them sopping duds." He gave Obie a shirt that hung past his knees and Bas overalls that had more holes than the roof of Bub Torrey's house. "Spread them overalls to dry, then set," he said and moved to the stove.

He filled three plates with a brownish looking stew that smelled spicy and sweet. He filled cups with coffee, pungent with chickory. "How you have it?" he asked. "Long or little sweeting?"

They asked for long and Bub pulled a crock from a shelf above the stove. He stuck his forefinger inside the jug of wild honey, swirled it around a few times until he had gathered a generous portion, then immersed his finger into the first, then second cup. "Me," he said with a sour smile, "I like mine short on the sweets."

Instead of honey, he took a chunk of brown sugar from a bowl, bit off half and dropped it into his cup. He removed the remaining piece from between his gums and

161

returned it to the bowl. "This here's bear meat," he explained and sat down on the opposite side of the wooden table. "Makes tasty eating with some ramps thrown in."

"Ramps?" Obie asked.

"Onions, boy. Where you say you was from?"

"Wilks Hollow. That's a half-day's walk northeast of Graysonia if you go by way of the road."

Bub Torrey nodded. He used a spoon to fill his mouth, the sleeve of his shirt to wipe his lips, a pointed finger to emphasize a point. "This here meal and putting you up overnight ought to be worth another four bits. You got cash-money, ain't you?"

Obie and Bas exchanged glances. "No sir, but I have something worth a lot more."

Obie left the table and returned with the packet of pearls from his overall pocket. Rather than opening it out of Bub Torrey's sight, he laid it on the table and folded back the cloth.

Bub Torrey's mouth fell open; food dropped out onto his whiskery chin. "Lord-a-mighty!" he whispered. As his eyes darted from the pearls to Obie's face, he said, "Thought you told me you was going to visit kin?"

Before Obie could respond, Torrey said, "You storied. You went to River Country." He reared back in his chair. "You two look a mite briar-scratched but better than most that come from that place. Times past I seen fellers come away from there that weren't ever right in the head again."

Bub Torrey sucked in a breath. "My brothers and two cousins went to River Country. Come home talking crazy. Told me they heard men screaming, smelled smoke when there weren't nobody there except them, saw Indian track and bear pads. My brother were sucked into the creek; near drowned, too. Weren't ever right in the head after that neither. Kept telling folks that he met the Immortals."

"Immortals?"

Bub Torrey nodded. "Queer happenings in that country."

Torrey's gaze narrowed as he studied Bas, then shifted his attention to Obie. "You see anything like what I just told?"

Obie moved stew from one side of his plate to the other. "Smelled smoke once that I couldn't explain."

"I smelled it, too," Bas said. "And I seen bear pads. Biggest dang things I ever looked on. Obie here fell in the creek. Made him swimmy headed for a spell."

Bub wiped the back of his hand across his chin. "A-body's lucky to come out of that place with his hide, let alone all them pearls. Must be that the Lord were a-looking after you."

Obie chose a medium-sized pearl and offered it in payment. But Bub Torrey threw up his hand. "Don't want no part of that thing."

"Sir, it's a real pearl. Worth a sight more than a dollar."

"Ain't doubting you, youngster, and it don't matter none if you owe me ten. You put them pretties back in your pocket." Bub pushed his empty plate into the center of the table. "Having it to look on might give me notions I'm too old to have. Don't need no more things than what I got."

Bub filled the boys' plates a second time, then sat back and watched Obie close the cloth over the pearls and slip them into the shirt pocket. When they finished eating, Bub gave them each a quilt. "Watch out for my corn," he said and offered Bas a candle.

Bas went up the ladder first. "This here loft is full of creepy-crawlers," he whispered. "The outdoors might be some better."

"It's dry, isn't it?"

"It's that but it gives me the wiggle-jiggles."

Bas raised the candle to show more of the loft. Cobwebs hung from the beams like decorations, dust thicker than flour, nests and a strange mixture of smells and sounds. Tobacco and moldy corn added their scents to the breeze creeping through the cracks. Obie rolled up in the old quilt and stretched the length of the husk-filled pallet.

"Obie," Bas whispered, "we ain't staying a minute past sunup even if our britches ain't dry."

Obie squeezed his eyes tight. Being inside was warmer; a roof over their heads did protect them from the damp night; it felt real welcome to be dry and warm. Yet Obie used his hands to press against his ears, to shut out the sounds of rats chewing, trees scraping against the tin roof. But no amount of thinking or pressing against his ears kept out the whispers, the whispers of the Nun Yuna Wi, faint and far off.

Obie rolled over. Had it really happened or was it all the simple result of being knocked unconscious? Obie knew about the Immortals . . . people who lived forever. He knew, too, that few living men ever saw an Immortal, that still fewer lived to tell about it. Had he really seen the Immortals, shared their food and visited their village?

Had they spared him for a special purpose?

Obie's eyelids rolled back. He believed that the idea to go to River Country and look for pearls came from God. He had lived with the strong feeling for days before telling his mamma.

"Your going over the mountain to River Country ain't got one thing to do with the Lord's will."

He kept telling her about the feeling, about waking up in the night and being aware of a strange presence in the room he shared with his brothers.

"Well," she finally said, *"I ain't one to tell you them feelin's you got is a bellyache. Only you know where they come from. Trust is what I got to tell you. Trust, and the Lord'll make everything clear in His own time."*

Obie mulled the happenings over in his mind. Why had he been saved from the sucking pot if it was wrong for him to go to Michigan? If it was the Lord's will, then his mamma would have to listen. But would she?

CHAPTER
14
✳ ✳ ✳

THEY LEFT BUB TORREY'S PLACE JUST AFTER SUNRISE, leaving behind a pearl for Torrey to find. With their still-soggy shoes thrown over their shoulders, they walked with new bounce. Even Chaser trotted ahead, working the edge of the scrub on both sides of the road.

Though the rain left it a mire of squish, it rambled through a stretch of rich bottom, dark as chocolate. Tobacco barns, and fields where the long-leaf crop grew, lay alongside; corn, days before ready for harvest, now lay pounded into the ground. Tucked back beyond the trees stood an occasional house with smoke and the scents of breakfast curling up from the chimney.

Obie knew that the pained look Bas wore had more to do with hunger than the breeze blowing against his wet pants. Obie admitted to the pinch in his belly, too. The thought of sitting down to his mamma's Sunday morning breakfast kept him company along the ribbon of road—

biscuits and cream gravy, grits and fried eggs, ham and venison, dewberry jelly and more biscuits, all of it washed down with cups of hot coffee, thickened with fresh cream.

Obie chewed on those thoughts for half a mile. The mercantile in Iversol would have nothing to match his mamma's cooking but it had things sure to fill an empty belly. "We're gonna trade another of our pearls for food," he told Bas, then glanced up at the ebony-hued crows circling overhead.

They passed an old church with broken windows and a fence falling down around the burying yard before Bas said, "Got to ask you something, Obie. It's been eating at me ever since I heard you say it."

The distant drone of an oncoming truck caught Bas's attention and made him turn his head. "This notion you got for going north, ain't it the real reason we went to River Country?"

An old truck rumbled over the hill, coasted down and splashed its way toward them. The driver slowed as he passed, waved and left behind the smell of hogs. "You know why I went to River Country," Obie said. "My daddy owes Arvis Cagley."

"I know that, but what I'm searching for is the whole truth."

They dropped over the crest of the hill. The bottom widened and cultivated fields reached back another few acres. "I told you the truth," Obie finally answered.

Asters and goldenrod continued to bloom but the rain's force had bent their stems and buried their blooms in the mud. "You don't think I would just walk off and leave my family with no way to pay their debts, do you?"

Obie resented Bas's insinuations; he resented the heaviness it left inside his chest. He resented the disbelief showing over Bas's broad face. "How come you don't believe me?"

"Ain't that I don't all-together believe you, it's that I can't figure you."

The warmth of the bright sun released the lemony odor of richweed into the air. "You say you want to be like your uncle Tully, 'cepting you can't be. There ain't a more selfish man living. He don't amount to a poot in a whirlwind."

"What are you talking about? You don't know my uncle."

"I know what your daddy told my daddy. Soon as Dalton took to the jug, his tongue started lapping like a hound dog's on a hot day."

"Well," Obie said, startled by the anger in his voice, "are you going to tell me what my daddy said or not?"

Bas shifted his shoes to the other shoulder. "Your uncle Tully borrowed money from your daddy to go north, borrowed more money from your uncle Hassel, up Thompson Creek way. When your uncle Hassel got in a fix, he wrote to your mother's brother, asking for the money back so's he could pay his taxes and money he owed the bank. Your uncle Tully wrote back that he didn't have it to spare. Told your daddy the same when he wrote for what was owed him."

Obie glared at Bas, his lips tightening into a hard, straight line. "I don't believe you."

"Don't go getting all crossways to what I'm telling you. I got no call to lie. And I'm only asking because I can't figure you wanting to be like him."

Obie hurried on; utter silence surrounded him. It was not true . . . Tully brought gifts to everyone, drove a new automobile, wore fine clothes and white shoes with shiny toes. Obie remembered the roll of money he pulled from his pocket when the plate was passed at church. He remembered staring at those white shoes and wanting to someday own such a pair.

It was lies, lies told by a man who drank too much. Tully had promised Obie a job; he was high up, had a whole passel of men working under him. *"Have more money than I can spend"* was what Obie remembered his uncle Tully saying. A high-up man would never lie about such things. And if he owed money, he would surely pay, especially if it was owed to kinfolk.

Obie glanced back at Bas. Lies!

Obie stopped. He waited for Bas to catch up. "When my daddy was drinking, he said lots of things. You heard the stories he told, heard him swear they were pure gospel. He even lied to Mamma when he took to the jug."

"Why would he tell my daddy such stories if they weren't true?"

"Hell," Obie snapped, "how should I know?"

But Obie suspected his daddy lied to save face, to put the blame for losing his land onto Tully's shoulders. His daddy was forever blaming others for his misfortunes. But a son's place was to keep still about his daddy's faults, and Obie jammed his hands deep inside his pockets.

His fingers touched the packet of pearls and closed around it. He took deep breaths to rid himself of the anger and reasoned that Bas had proven to be a friend. He had no reason to lie. Obie looked out; he took in everything surrounding him—the listless green look of the oak leaves, the scrub turning brown, the leafless ivy vines sunning themselves.

Obie remembered his granddaddy telling that inside every dying thing was already a growing seed for its rebirth the coming spring. All that Obie saw before him testified to a world fast falling asleep. Obie scrunched his shoulders up around his ears. Sun warmed his backside and promised to dry his shoes. They were his only pair and he needed them for the trip north.

The boys walked on, neither speaking. Yet Obie felt the pressure to say something. He had spoken hastily, angrily, but it was not until they were at the mercantile in Iversol that Obie said, "I'm sorry; I know you told the truth. Sometimes my daddy was less than honorable; that's why he said those things about Uncle Tully."

They left Chaser and their wet shoes outside the store. A large-faced wall clock read half-past nine. The only person inside wore eyeglasses and elastic arm bands to hold up the sleeves of his white shirt. "Morning," he said. "You boys find your way to Fraser's Crossing?"

Obie hesitated while trying to decide whether to be truthful or tell the storekeeper another lie. Was he a fair man or would he try to take advantage? "No, sir," Obie replied, "when the rain started we turned back. Like to have never gotten here with the rivers running so high."

"Farther east a feller goes, the worse things get. Up nawth, along them big rivers, lots of folks lost everything."

Obie moved closer to the counter and took a deep breath of the smells held inside the walls. His gaze leaped from one corner of the room to another as he removed a pearl from his pocket. He stretched his arm across the counter and uncurled his fingers, taking careful note of the expression on the storekeeper's face. "My friend and I would like to trade this pearl for some eats."

The storekeeper looked down. His lips worked silently, like someone adding numbers in a slow, methodical way. Behind the wire-framed glasses, brown eyes narrowed beneath thick brows. Slowly his head moved from side to side. "That's as handsome a pearl as I've seen." He took it between his thumb and forefinger, held it up to the light. "Ain't gonna ask where you found it or how many others you got; most folk like to keep them things private, but I think we can strike a fair bargain."

He removed a handkerchief from his pocket and placed the pearl on it. "You boys help yourselves to whatever you want. Set the things here, alongside the pearl. When we're both satisfied with our bargain, I'll take the pearl and you take the food."

Obie's chest swelled with the pleasure of his bargain while Bas set a tin of crackers on the counter. He asked for raisins and a thick wedge of yellow cheese. Obie added two cans of peaches, two cans of pork and beans, four bottles of strawberry soda, then asked for a sack of jellied orange slices. He could already taste the sweetness stick to his teeth, curl up on the back of his tongue and melt down his throat. The storekeeper added four apples to the boys' cache without being asked, a generous amount of smoked venison strips, a half dozen chocolate bars, a can opener and four Moon Pies.

"How far is home?" he asked.

"A ways east of Graysonia."

The storekeeper stroked his chin before taking a half dozen hard-cooked eggs from a jar and pickled pigs' feet from another. "That ought to hold you."

Obie glanced at Bas for a sign. His big grin confirmed his satisfaction. "Sir, I have a dog outside and she's a real fine animal. Suppose you could throw in something for her? I'd be happy . . ."

The storekeeper waved Obie silent. He stepped out back and a few minutes later returned with a joint of fresh meat. "All this rain brought the deer out of the hills," he explained. "Shot two big buck right off my back step."

"I'm obliged," Obie said. "You've been more than fair."

The storekeeper grinned, showing his pink gums. "Got boys of my own," he said. "Never seen the likes to what they can eat."

He folded his handkerchief around the pearl. "I thank you," he said. "I'm gonna save this for Christmas and give it to my missus. Only nice thing I ever give her was a pretty lace shawl but it was secondhand."

He helped load the boys' arms and walked them to the door. "If you younguns want to hook up with a long ride, you best sashay your bottoms down to the highway." He pointed west. "When you come on the first fork-turn, take the left-hand prong. No more than a hoot-an'-holler from there."

"Thanks," Obie called back. "Thanks a lot."

Chaser jumped up, planting her paws on Obie's shoulder and licking his face. Bas kicked their shoes along as they moved around to the side of the building. Before they settled on a place to eat, Chaser began barking, jumping on her hind feet and acting like a pup. "I best give her the bone before she breaks her fool neck," Obie said and threw it a few feet off.

Bas sat cross-legged beneath the hickory, surveyed all the food before he smiled. "My," he said, "this here reminds me of the candy pie supper at the Baptist Church last Fourth of July."

"There'll be bigger and better celebrations than that soon as we get home and show folks what we got."

They ate cheese and crackers and raisins while Bas opened cans and bottles. Without spoons they poured the beans and peaches into their mouths. Bas sucked the pigs' feet clean and drank a bottle of strawberry soda without stopping. "My belly—" he laughed "—thinks it's gone to heaven."

Obie peeled the hard-boiled eggs. He threw one to Chaser, shared his half of the smoked venison with her, too, then fell back onto his elbows. "I'm full," he said, "full to my gizzard."

But Bas continued to eat. He emptied his cans and ate the remainder of Obie's beans. They divided the rest of the food, stashed it in their pockets, then cleaned up their mess and returned the empty soda bottles to the store before moving on.

The first logger to pass stopped and carried them as far as the Tarnight Mill. Nearly two hours passed before a W.P.A. truck came by and hauled them north to the Graysonia junction.

Alongside the road and finishing off the last candy bars and Moon Pies, they debated their chances of catching a ride into Graysonia or cutting off over the ridge for Wilks Hollow. "It'll save six miles if we go over Bales Ridge," Obie said. "Even then it's gonna be long past dark before we get there. But you're welcome to spend the night."

"Your mamma told me to never set foot on her land if I valued my hide. I do believe she meant every word."

173

"You're a good friend, Bas. And I intend to tell her all that you've done for us. What happened to Daddy wasn't anyone's fault except his. She's got to bring herself to accept that."

Before setting off over the ridge. Obie divided the pearls. He wrapped his thirty-three in the scrap of cloth torn from the tail of his shirt. He pushed the packet deep inside his pocket before letting out a slow, satisfied sigh. "It sure is good to be looking at home country 'stead of all that wilderness."

CHAPTER

15

✻ ✻ ✻

OBIE STOPPED, OUT OF BREATH AND PANTING WHEN HE reached the top of Addie's Ridge. Instead of starting down immediately, he paused. He whistled for Chaser to come back but she smelled home and ran ahead. Off to the north, Felker Mountain stood out strong against the moonlit sky. Below and a short way beyond the meadow, a single light shone from inside the cabin. His mamma would be in front of the stove, rocking, her eyes closed and nursing Loranda.

It looked exactly as he remembered, yet different. And the difference he compared to shoes . . . wear a pair to school every day, go barefoot the whole summer, put shoes back on in the fall and they feel like strangers. And that was how Obie felt . . . like a stranger.

"You sure it's gonna be all right?" A pleading flavored Bas's tone. "I can sleep in the barn; be gone before daylight; your mamma don't need to know."

"But she should know what you've done. You didn't have to go with me. And you had cause to leave me there more than once."

Bas shrugged thick shoulders. "I owed you Wilks. I'm the one that give your daddy his last jug."

"But it wasn't your fault that his thirst caused him to wreck the truck."

Obie turned toward home. "Come on, Bas. I got a real need for my own bed."

Obie knew the southerly slope of Addie's Ridge as well as his name. He remembered his daddy and grand-daddy cutting chestnut trees, which they later hand-hewed and turned into timbers for the barn and summer-kitchen. Obie swung himself over the split-rail fence on two hands. Home . . . the only one he knew. Realizing how close they came to losing it and the changes that would have caused made Obie swallow hard. And the pain stayed with him across the meadow, past the spring-house.

He heard Chaser barking, saw his mamma standing in the open doorway. Her hand pressed against her fore-head as if that would help her to see. "Mamma," Obie yelled, "Mamma, I'm home."

"Obie? Obie, that you? Lord-a-mercy," she exclaimed, "I near worried myself to death not knowing if you was dead or what. Hurry, Son. Let me rest these sorry eyes on you."

Chaser ran back to meet him, barked, then spun around and followed him the rest of the way. "I'm all right, Mamma. Tired and briar-scratched, but I'm fine. Real fine."

Obie leaped from the ground to the porch, grabbed

his mamma and hugged her. "I followed great-gran'-daddy's map, Mamma. Found the mussel beds, too. It wasn't no pie-in-the-sky notion. No, sir!"

But before Obie could tell her about the pearls, he felt her body stiffen. "What's he doin' here?" she asked, as the warmth left her voice.

"Bas is here because I asked him. He went to River Country with me, Mamma. He saved my life. If it hadn't—"

She broke into Obie's explanation. "You ain't welcome here. I told you that. Told you I'd shoot you dead if you ever set foot on Wilks's land again."

"Mamma—"

She turned on Obie. Her face was hidden in shadows but her anger was plain as she yelled, "Them devils and their poison took your daddy from me."

"Not so, Mamma, and you have to stop blaming the Allardices. It was Daddy that drove up Felker Mountain to get a jug. It was his choice to drink it. Wrecking the truck and getting himself killed had nothing to do with Bas or his daddy. If you have to blame someone, Mamma, blame the man you married."

Obie turned to invite Bas inside but the night was busy with its own sounds and Bas had disappeared. "Good riddance!" Mattie Mae hissed. "The devil take all them Allardices."

Obie followed her inside. A faint yellow light shone out from the lantern. Warmth filled the kitchen and the lingering odor of steam-softened shuck beans. Before Obie could speak to the younguns, his mamma shooed Josh and Delsie back to bed. Obie started to object but he recognized the set of his mamma's jaw and knew the uselessness of arguing. It surprised him, too, that the others slept through the racket. Or had they?

Obie closed the door while his mamma returned to her rocker. She lifted Loranda from the oven door and returned the infant to her arms. Sensing that he had gotten off on the wrong foot and hoping to make amends, Obie crouched beside her. He studied the deep lines beneath her sunken eyes, her sallow skin and stained teeth. It was a face that years ago may have been pretty, though always determined. He remained beside her, aware of the strained silence yet content to listen to Loranda's tiny blue lips suckle his mamma's breast. Finally Obie whispered, "Mamma, I found the pearls I went to find. Got thirty-three right here in my pocket."

She continued to rock without giving any sign of responding. Obie withdrew the packet of pearls, folded back the flannel cloth and held it out for her to see. "Look, Mamma, aren't they pretty? Look what I found."

She opened her eyes. Pink, blue, lavender, peach, green, gold . . . a rainbow of soft pastels. Obie smiled, expecting a favorable response. After all, he had done it for her, saved her from losing the land, from being sent to the poor farm and her children to an orphanage. He had done it for her, yet the space between them overflowed with silence.

Obie regarded his mamma with a mixture of anger and hurt. He knew of her condition, her moods. Again Obie remembered his daddy saying. *"She's got a face for every one."* And Mattie Mae Wilks did. Sweet-like at Lester Quade's store; on Sunday and Wednesday evening church meetings it was a saintly silence that some folks called pious; helpless, even pitiful when she was scheming to get her way. But when none of her moods brought her what she wanted, she dredged up a look that dripped with gall. She wore that mood now and Obie groped for a reason.

He had done the expected thing, taken hold in his daddy's place. "Mamma"—Obie laid the thirty-three pearls on the blanket that covered Loranda—"what is it you want of me?"

Her lips drew tight against her teeth. Her blue eyes glared at him below the stringy dull hair that hung around her thin, bony face. She stopped short of saying *all that I can get,* but Obie read it on her lips. Then in a voice cold as frost, she said, "There's butchering to be done, meat that needs smoking; barn roof leaks like a sieve, root cellar's falling in, fence is down. Selena and Caleb got the diarrhea; corn ain't been shucked. Timber needs cutting, hauled down and chopped, else we'll freeze to death come winter. Ain't you the oldest? Ain't looking after things your job?"

As Obie moved the packet of pearls to the wooden table, he said, "Those same things needed doing before Daddy passed on last August."

"You calling your daddy a no-account? He was off working hisself to death so you could get your schooling."

Obie felt the weight of guilt. "Mamma, Virg and Orvull live here, too. They're not helpless."

"You telling me you're too good to help out? You over fatted on all that book learning, Obie?"

"No." Obie shifted his weight. "It's just that I . . ."

"You're going somewheres, I know it. Found road

maps stuffed under your mattress. That's why you went looking for pearls, ain't it?"

She leaned forward. "You're fixing to run off. I know it well as I know my name."

Obie reached over and tucked the blanket around Loranda's bare foot before he responded. "I'm not going to lie, Mamma. There are enough pearls here to pay off the family's debts and extra for you. The rest I'm using to pay my way north."

Mattie Mae hunched her thin shoulders as she leaned over the baby to confront her son with bitter eyes. "That schoolteacher put them notions in your head, didn't she? I told your daddy no good would come from that nawthern woman."

"Mrs. Middleton's not northern. Her kin came from the Cumberland."

"Went to school in the nawth, didn't she? Married a nawthern man, didn't she? Mrs. Middleton, Mrs. Middleton, Mrs. Middleton." Each time she repeated the schoolteacher's name the twang grew nastier. "You don't know that woman from Adam's cat yet you let her turn you against your own kin."

"Mamma, no one's trying to turn me against you."

"What I'm saying, Obadiah, is that you take on about that nawthern woman like she hung the moon and stars. And I'm sick to death hearing about her."

Obie never knew his mother to dislike anyone the way she disliked Mrs. Middleton, disliked her before ever laying eyes on her. "It's not Mrs. Middleton that got me to thinking about going north. It was your brother." Obie leaned back onto his heels. "You remember the time Uncle Tully came here, driving that new blue roadster and wearing those fancy white shoes?"

Mattie Mae's face went flat. Weeks of fatigue crowded in.

"Uncle Tully told me that if I should ever want to come north, he'd help me get started. He said he would get me a job where he works. He told me, Mamma, that he was real high up."

"Whatcha want to go nawth for? Nothing up there."

"I want things like Uncle Tully has. I want to be high up. I want people's respect. I get dang tired of Virg beating me bloody. I'm sick of being poor. Do you know what folks in town say about us, Mamma?" Without giving her time to respond, he blurted, "They say us folks up Wilks Hollow is too poor to paint and too proud to whitewash. They call us poor-whites, Mamma. We ain't even good enough to be called rednecks."

Obie stood. He backed off, jammed both fists into his pockets. He hadn't meant to get so talkative, so honest. He felt his belly twisting, felt the heat boil up into his head, turn his face red. *Being poor and a nobody was worse than being dead. He was going north. Gonna make something of himself!*

Obie returned to his mother's side, knelt down and took a deep breath to steady himself before he began again. "Mamma," he said, "I heard that Uncle Tully borrowed money from Daddy and Uncle Hassel so he could go north. I heard that Uncle Hassel and Daddy both wrote him and asked for that money so they could pay their debts. I heard that Uncle Tully wrote back, saying he didn't have it to spare. Is that true, Mamma?"

She laughed a high-pitched screech that awakened Loranda and caused her to cry. "Now look what you went and done."

"Mamma, is it true?"

Mattie Mae raised the infant to her shoulder, rubbed the thin, fragile back until the child quieted. "Your daddy could barely write his own name much less a whole letter."

"I know, Mamma. I know that if such a letter was written, you wrote it."

"Who told you such mean lies?"

"Bas said that Daddy told Mr. Allardice one night when he got to drinking."

"Lies. Lies told by liars! Them Allardices is trash, sinners against the good Lord."

The muscles around her eyes jiggled. She looked about in quick nervous jerks. Obie raised his elbows to his knees and blew into his fists. Was Dalton Wilks the liar and Bas had only repeated the lie? Or was Mattie Mae the liar?

Obie felt the weight of not knowing seep through his pores, into his flesh. His blood absorbed it, carried it through his body, leaving it to settle in the bowels of his being. He rose slowly from his place beside her. He eased his hand beneath the packet of pearls on the table. He carried them to the can shelf in the corner of the kitchen and took down the mason jar. He unscrewed the lid, dropped the packet inside with the deed to their land, marriage license and birth certificates, then closed the lid tight. He walked to the door, took a coat from the peg, put it on.

"Where you going?" she asked. "Obadiah Wilks, answer me, you hear?"

Obie stepped outside. He closed the door on her demands. He felt Chaser beside him and he reached down. "Mamma's having one of her moods. It's her condition." And Obie slanted off toward the barn.

CHAPTER
16
✳ ✳ ✳

AS DAYLIGHT'S FIRST SIGNAL STRETCHED OUT ALONG THE eastern rim of Addie's Ridge, old Stonewall began his morning ritual of stretching his scrawny neck its length, flapping both wings and crowing. The sound swirled up from the deepest part of his belly and burst forth into the crisp morning. He strutted past the barn door, across the yard as if his assigned duty was to awaken everyone still asleep.

Obie rested on his side and watched through the open door. Stonewall reminded him of Virg the way he pranced up and down, acting important, contributing nothing except noise. If he had a say in the old bird's future it would be to wring his scrawny neck. But he doubted that the old rooster would make a fit stew.

Obie crawled out from under a layer of straw. Beside Chaser, watching, Silas blew out his thick lips and swished his tail. "Too bad about you," Obie said, and slipped a halter over Silas's ears.

Obie knew his mamma was up and about, smelled smoke before he saw it curling up from the chimney. He knew he needed to make her understand that his going north would be good for the family. Hiding the road map under his mattress had been stupid, especially with his route to Michigan outlined with blue Crayola. No wonder she thought so poorly of him and his pearls. He turned Silas out to pasture, fed the goats, grained the chickens. He cut kindling next, hauled wood to fill the box before returning to the house. "Morning," he said, picking up the milk bucket, empty water pail, and hurrying back outside.

Obie knew his mamma to go for days without talking. Just like Stonewall, she had a ritual that called for her head to tilt back, chin out, mouth curled down, her eyes always challenging, never putting to rest the thing upsetting her. She spoke of herself as a forgiving woman; Obie knew her to have a good heart. Except she never forgot, especially those things that went against her will or those things he did. That puzzled Obie, too. Puzzled him because Virg was always being thoughtless and never doing what she asked of him. He even called her a nag, right to her face, and she let on like it was funning.

After the cows were grained, milked and turned out with Silas, Obie filled the water bucket and returned to the house. "Everything is done, Mamma." He set the milk pail on the stool. "I'm going in to Graysonia and pay off Daddy's debt soon as I clean myself."

She stood over the stove, continuing to stir the pot of mush.

"Want me to wake the kids, Mamma?"

She made no effort to respond. Obie raised a hand

and started to reason with her but shrugged instead. He opened the door to the bare-walled bedroom that he shared with his brothers and the smell of Caleb's pee.

Virg had taken over the big bed Obie shared with Josh, put Josh on the floor next to Orvull's pallet. Obie awakened his little brother first, then shook the shoulders of the other two. "Go call your sisters, Josh. Mamma's cooking breakfast."

There were nine Wilks children. Delsie, the first girl; Orrie came next; Josh, Caleb and Selena were short stair steps. Loranda, wrapped in a blanket, lay on the oven door while the others took their places at the table.

"Lord," Mattie Mae folded her hands and bowed her head, "me and the younguns thank You for this food, the roof over us, the bounty from this land that fills our cellar. I know, Lord, that I been a-pesterin' for a miracle that would pay off all we owe and enough to see us through hard times. I thank You, Lord, for sending me them thirty-three pearls in answer to my prayers. Amen," Mattie Mae finished, and the youngsters joined in.

Delsie spoke first, wanting to see the pearls; Josh asked about the Nun Yuna Wi and River Country; Orvull snickered over the possibility of there being a cave or sucking pot that took men down into the land of the Immortals; Virg asked to hold the pearls, asked if there were really thirty-three, but Mattie Mae shushed them quiet, saying, " 'Pears to me you're all being more interested in the getting than you are in the thanking. Them thirty-three pearls up there on the can shelf is the Lord's answer to all the prayers I been a-saying. It was Him that sent them to me."

Virg looked at Obie from the side, then his gaze

wandered toward the can shelf, while Mattie Mae's choice of words added fuel to Obie's anger. Was it her intent to claim all thirty-three pearls?

"Delsie," she said, "I need you to stay to home today and watch the little ones while Obie takes me to Graysonia to settle up your daddy's debt."

"But, Mamma, I can't. Mrs. Middleton's giving a real important quiz. I can't miss it."

Mattie Mae pressed both hands flat to the table. "Seems to me that you and your brother care more for that nawthern woman than you do for your own mamma." Mattie Mae drummed her fingers. "You'll stay to home, Delsie Jean, like I say."

Delsie lowered her head. "Yes, Mamma."

Through the rest of the meal no one spoke or looked up from the breakfast of biscuits and gravy. But the sounds of eating and Loranda's whimpering pushed Obie into a corner. This was his family; he knew that being the oldest gave him certain responsibilities. He felt the weight of those responsibilities; they went deep, like taproots, and bound him to Wilks Hollow.

Obie looked at his sisters, his brothers. He looked at his mamma until she glanced up and caught him staring. He turned away but promised himself he'd take those few leftover pearls and travel north just as he had planned. After all, he found the pearls, went hungry, risked his life to get them home. If they were truly the Lord's gift, then the Lord had put them in his hands, not his mamma's. Seemed only right that a small share belonged to him.

He waited until Mattie Mae shooed the others off to get ready for school before he said, "Mrs. Middleton told me, before I went to River Country, that soon as I got back home she would drive the pearls to Nashville for me. A man named Mr. Aaron Smith is paying twenty dollars each for good pearls. But we don't have the time for her to do that. Daddy's note is due tomorrow."

Obie focused his eyes on the oilcloth table cover. "Mr. Cagley will likely offer less than what the pearls are worth, seventeen maybe. We owe him one hundred and eighty-seven dollars, Mamma, including interest; that's eleven pearls."

He glanced up but her intimidating stare sent his gaze shooting off into the corner of the room. "I plan on taking twelve pearls to get me started up north, so there will be ten left over. I know Mrs. Middleton will take the pearls we have left to Nashville and get us twenty dollars each."

Obie felt his mamma's silent rage boil up between them. Yet he went on: "You'll be left with two hundred dollars, Mamma."

Mattie Mae chose to continue rocking, to remain silent, to stare through Obie. He pushed back the bench finally and helped Delsie stack dishes. Filling the washpan with boiling water, feeling the steam rise up in his face added to his anger and he whirled about. "There's good tableland farther up the holler, fine for grazing cattle. With the money you have left over, you should think on buying a few heifer calves. That'll give you a start at building your own herd. That's what Mr. Cagley and the others with extra dollars are doing."

"Delsie," Mattie Mae said, "tell your brother to get hisself cleaned. Ain't going to town with nobody looking like him. You kin tell him to get Silas from the pasture, too."

"Mamma, listen to me," Obie pleaded. "All I'm asking for is a chance. I got something important to do with my life."

"You saying we ain't important?"

"No, that's not what I'm saying. My going north will be good for this family. I'll send money regular. Come to visit as often as I can."

Mattie Mae's eyes drilled through his. Finally she said, "You got no more coming to you than what I say. Now go fetch Silas."

"Obie," Josh called from the open door, "want me to fetch him?"

Obie backed off from his mother's stare. He let the door swing shut before he spun on his toes and dropped over three steps to the ground.

"Did you see real Indians? Did you get caught in a sucking pot? Did you—"

"Shut up, Josh! Shut up and leave me be."

But Josh trailed along behind, kicking at the dirt with the toes of his shoes, skipping a rock across the meadow. "How come you're not off to school?" Obie asked.

"Virg ain't ready."

"What about Orvull and the girls? They left; they're down by the corn field. If you hurry you might catch up."

"Can't."

"Why not?"

" 'Cause Orvull won't let me walk with him no more."

"Since when?"

"Since I told Mamma that him and Johnny Bob Quade had a jug out behind the schoolhouse privy."

Obie sprang over the split-rail fence. "Orvull the cause of that knot on your head?"

Josh nodded. "He ain't near so brave 'less Virg is around. Just blows a lot of hot air out of his big mouth. Obie, can I walk with you and Mamma as far as school?"

"Nope." Obie whistled for Silas. "She's in one of her moods. Besides, me and her got talking to do."

"She was real sick while you was gone. Doc come; told her to get to bed." Josh followed Obie across the meadow. "She told Doc she were skeered you run off, that you were never coming home again."

Obie led Silas toward the gate. "Was Mamma sick with the grippe?"

Josh shook his head. "Doc told Delsie it had to do with the new baby coming."

"Loranda doesn't look good either. Doc say anything about her?"

"Said she were a blue baby." Josh opened the gate. "That's 'cause of her being that blue color and always a-crying."

"She going to die?"

Josh shrugged.

After Obie tied Silas to the fence, he said, "You best be getting down the road before you're late."

"I told you I was waiting on Virg." Josh grinned. "He told everyone at school that you'd not be coming home. He told Mamma that you were sure to run off if you found anything worth keeping."

Obie took the porch steps two at a time. "I'll tell Virg that you're waiting."

The kitchen stood empty, the table, too. Obie glanced up at the mason jar resting in its usual place on the can shelf. He started for it. But his mamma had an impatient streak. So he turned and took fresh clothes from the bureau drawer.

Virg was sitting on the edge of the bed when Obie opened the door. "Josh is waiting on you," he said, and peeled down to his underwear.

"It true that you found thirty-three pearls, that you brung them home and stuck them in that mason jar for Mamma to use?"

"Found sixty-eight," Obie said. "Bas took thirty-three and we traded two."

"How come you to come back? I wouldn't have. I'd be gone so fast nobody would see my dust."

"I came back because Mamma needs the money." Obie left his dirty overalls on the floor.

He drew a pan of fresh water from the well. He scrubbed all over with the gritty yellow soap. He felt good about himself, about bringing the pearls home, about doing something honorable, something Virg would never have done.

Virg hurried out of the house, jumped over the steps, took off running. "Bye, Obie," Josh called and raced after his brother.

Obie dried off before returning to the bedroom. The clean clothes felt soft against his skin, smelled sweet, like fresh cut hay. He slipped his feet inside the stiff shoes, wishing he could go barefoot. But his mamma would throw a screaming fit if he were to walk into Mr. Arvis Cagley's office without shoes.

"Obie," Delsie called, "Mamma's waiting."

"I'll fetch Silas," he said, noticing Delsie take down the mason jar and reach inside for the packet of pearls.

When he returned from the barn he helped his mamma up onto Silas's broad back and led the mule along the deeply rutted road until reaching the branch creek. Obie picked his way across the rocky bed carefully, then turned toward town.

"Mamma, I know you're not feeling well. I know that my going north is a real disappointment. But I give you my word, I'll come home real often, help out whenever I can."

Brownish-red earth stained the toes of Obie's shoes. "It's important, Mamma, that I know the truth about Uncle Tully. Did he borrow money, then refuse to pay it back? Did he do that?"

Mattie Mae's chin shot out. She turned aside and gave every indication that she intended to ignore his question. "Them Allardices is liars," she hissed. "My brother is a good boy, always has been. His whole life, folks have been a-backbiting his good name. Jealous of his good looks and fine manners, that's why they're always a-faulting him."

"*Tully Crumpler could charm a snake back into its hole,*" was what Dalton Wilks used to say about his brother-in-law. But was that a good thing or bad? Obie couldn't decide. He wanted to believe his mamma. He wanted to believe that Bas had repeated a lie, wanted to believe that Tully Crumpler was an honorable man, high-up and respected.

Obie tied Silas behind Lester Quade's store, helped his mamma down and reached out to take her arm, except she pulled away. She smoothed back her hair, smoothed down the front of her cotton dress, smoothed the wrinkles from the back of her coat. Without a single word, she stepped past Obie, waited at the edge of the street for a lumber truck to pass, then crossed toward Arvis Cagley's real estate office.

Obie wondered what she would do if he refused to follow her. He decided she would do nothing since she had the pearls and he rushed ahead to open the door. She stepped inside without breaking stride.

Mr. Arvis Cagley's office took up the downstairs front of a large, two-story frame house that sat back from the street and behind a broad apron of grass. Obie closed the door.

Mr. Cagley looked up. Surprise spread across his face, then a slight smile. He stood, came from his rolltop desk, stretched his hand out to Mattie Mae and said all the polite things, like how well she looked when she looked more poorly than a cur dog with the mange.

Mattie Mae sat down in the chair he offered. It was obvious to Obie that Arvis Cagley suspected they were there to ask for more time. "I come," Mattie Mae began, "to settle up my mister's debt, and take back the paper to my land."

Arvis Cagley's mouth fell ajar.

Mattie Mae reached into her pocket and withdrew the packet. "I—"

But Obie interrupted his mamma. He explained his trip to River Country, finding the pearls and using them to pay off his daddy's debt. At first Arvis Cagley was noticeably reluctant until Obie took the packet from his mamma's hand and folded back the cloth. "They're nearly all perfect," Obie said. But instead of thirty-three pearls Obie counted twenty.

He wrenched around to accuse his mamma of taking

the others, but her eyes focused on the realtor. "That schoolteacher woman told me herself," Mattie Mae began, "that these would bring twenty dollars or more in Nashville. She said you'd likely offer seventeen. If that's fair to you it suits me."

Arvis Cagley's eyes shifted back and forth between the pearls and Mattie Mae Wilks as he weighed her offer. Obie suspected he would reject it, bicker at least. After all, this was the man that his mamma said would skin a flea for its hide and tallow.

But Arvis Cagley turned to his desk. He withdrew the note Dalton Wilks signed when he bought the truck for hauling logs. Across the front he scribbled: paid in full. He dated it, signed his name. "Mrs. Wilks," he began, "the nine pearls left—

"Nine?" Her head swung around. She glared at Obie through narrowed and piercing eyes.

"Yes, nine. If you would consider selling them, I'd consider buying them. For the right price, of course."

Her head turned slowly back. She studied the realtor, this man who folks said still had the first dollar he ever made. A slight smile quivered her lips. "Of course," she said. "Them nine I got left is thirty dollars each."

Thirty dollars each? Obie blinked. Was his mamma crazy? Why would she go and say thirty when she knew that Mrs. Middleton could get no more than twenty in Nashville?

Arvis Cagley balked at her demands, nearly laughed in her face before he lifted the biggest pearl to the light. He examined each of the remaining eight just as carefully while his tongue worked against his cheek. It was plain to see that Mr. Arvis Cagley wanted the pearls but dealing with the likes of Mattie Mae Wilks was next to an insult. "Well," the realtor said, "These are terrible hard times for us all, but Dalton were a friend of mine. Guess I can see myself clear to help out his widow." Arvis Cagley stuck out his hand.

Mattie Mae looked at it. For a moment Obie thought his mamma might refuse to shake hands. But she finally took the realtor's hand, pumped it up and down like it was a handle. "I weren't born behind no barn," she said. "I knowd who was friends with my mister, knowd, too, when I been bested."

She turned to Obie and added. "But I know how to do some besting myself."

She counted the money, counted it twice, folded the bills in half, and pushed them into her pocket before bidding Arvis Cagley a good day.

Obie followed his mamma outside. He didn't know whether to compliment her on her bargain or accuse her of stealing his pearls. Before he could decide she turned on him. Words flew past her lips in an unstoppable volley. Then they drew tight across her teeth. The skin around the eyes and over the forehead tightened, too, making her long, thin face into an angry mask, accusing him with the same venom as her words. But Obie knew his mamma, knew of her cleverness and ways she had of getting just what she wanted. She took the pearls all right, hid them somewheres.

He helped her up onto Silas's back, then led the mule along the road toward home. Might take a few days, he promised himself, but he'd find the other thirteen pearls, find where she hid them and leave Wilks Hollow forever.

CHAPTER

17

✳ ✳ ✳

OBIE FINISHED THE CHORES EARLY. RATHER THAN RETURN-ing to the house, he dropped down under the apple tree and chewed on one blade of grass after another. He thought about his pearls, about his mamma and her con-niving ways. He thought about the Immortals and tried to decide why they had set him free. What had been their reasons? What if their reasons went against what he wanted? Did he have a choice?

"Obie," Josh called, "come see what Mrs. Middleton sent you."

Obie looked out at the land, followed it up toward the high meadow where long shadows stretched across the green. Beyond the ridge lay miles and miles of road that reached all the way north to Michigan. Obie sucked on a back tooth. What if their reasons went against what he wanted? What if the thing he wanted—?

"Obie," Josh called from the porch, "Mamma wants you right now."

What if the thing he wanted . . . Dammit! His going to Michigan was a good thing. Bettering himself was what the Immortals had saved him for. It was! Obie finally pulled himself up, strolled back toward the house. Each step deepened his determination to have it out with her, demand that she return his pearls, tear the house up looking for them if she refused. Obie kicked the ground; a rock flew out ahead of him.

"Lookie," Josh said, when Obie stepped inside. "Mrs. Middleton sent you books to read before school on Monday."

History, arithmetic . . .

"Josh," Mattie Mae asked, "where's Virg?"

But Josh went on opening and closing Obie's school books. "Josh," Mattie Mae barked, "where's your brother? You deaf or you need your ears scrubbed?"

Delsie pushed Josh aside. "I bet he's up to Cora Sue Webster's. He's sweet on her, Mamma."

"Ain't so," Josh said, choosing an apple from the bowl and polishing it on the sleeve of his shirt. "Virg ain't coming."

Mattie Mae turned from the stove, the heel of her hand rested on a hip. "Whatcha mean, ain't coming?"

Josh bit into the apple; juice dribbled down his chin and onto his shirt. "Virg weren't in school the whole day, Mamma. Soon as we got to the creek, he waved down a logging truck. Told the driver he was going to California."

"California? California, you say?"

"That's what he told the driver. Said he was never gonna come back neither. Said he hated this place and all them in it. That's what he said, Mamma. I heared him clear." Josh hurriedly caught his breath. "Virg run off, Mamma. Sure as buzzards eat skunk, Virg run off."

Mattie Mae glanced at Obie while he studied her blue eyes. He tried reading the thoughts that made her chin quiver. Even her hand took to shaking, causing the spoon to rattle against the iron kettle. Slowly, the frown that had soured her face the whole day began to disappear. Her voice softened, too. "If you're telling another of your stories, Joshua Wilks, I'll take a strap to your bottom."

"I ain't storying, Mamma. I seen Virg reach in his pocket and pull out one of them pearls Obie brought home. He give it to the trucker for hauling him to Nashville." Josh plopped down on the bench, planted both elbows on the table. "Virg Wilks got up in that truck, slammed the door and spit out the window. Never looked back at me, said good-bye or nothing. He just rode off like a jackass going to its supper."

Mattie Mae turned and faced Obie. "It were Virg who done it," she whispered. "It were Virgil Dean."

A sudden, unexpected smile broke across her face. She waved the cooking spoon in Josh's face. "I'm gonna fix something real special for supper to celebrate what Obie here did for this family. Your daddy would be so proud. Dalton always said it were Obie here that were the responsible one."

"Yeah," Obie muttered, "and look what it got me."

Mattie Mae's smile disappeared; the warm fragrant air turned static. Obie, suddenly conscious of the words that had slipped past his lips, felt caught. Trapped between his dream to leave and the unseen powers that tied him to Wilks Hollow. Had the Nun Yuna Wi won after all? Was there no escaping his mamma and her younguns, this place he called home?

"Obie," Mattie Mae called. "Obadiah, where you a-going?"

Obie ran from the house, let the door slam shut. He ignored his mamma and the steps. He jumped to the ground. He ran past the springhouse, past the chicken pen, past the barn. He ran and Chaser ran alongside until they reached the top of Addie's Ridge.

Obie dropped to his knees, gulping in mouthfuls of air. "Dammit," he shouted. "It's not fair."

Obie closed his eyes, rested his forehead in his hands. "Lord," he cried out, "how could You let that lying, low-down no-account get away with my pearls? I trusted You."

Obie jumped up. He whirled around, crying loudly now, flinging his arms out as if to strike at the invisible. "How come, Lord? How come You to do this to me? You knew I was going north. You knew it!"

Obie dropped back to his knees. Tears filled his eyes and spilled onto his face as he looked from one end of Wilks Hollow to the other. "Lord, I don't understand, what is it that You want of me?"

Obie searched the length of Wilks Hollow. "There's nothing here to learn. How come You're always favoring Virg? You made him bigger, stronger. You let him get away with everything and me with nothing. It's not fair, Lord!"

Obie threw a rock. He watched it roll down the hillside, bounce off other rocks, then skip in different directions before it stopped. "I got no idea what You have in mind for me. But it's not what I had in mind for

198

myself." He crossed one leg over the other; his chest quivered.

His gaze followed the meadow down to the house, then across to the pond. He felt like one of the fish trapped there, spending its whole life swimming in the same small circle. No amount of jumping or twisting or praying would ever get him shed of that pond. No way that fish was ever gonna be free again.

Obie felt that way, too.

CHAPTER

18

✳ ✳ ✳

OBIE SKIPPED CHURCH ON SUNDAY; EVEN TURNED A DEAF ear on all of his mamma's nagging and dire predictions. Didn't matter to him one bit if the Lord struck Virg Wilks dead. Wouldn't matter none if the Lord Himself struck him dead. Wouldn't matter if the Nun Yuna Wi shot burning pine splinters through his heart. Being dead would be better than spending the rest of his life up Wilks Hollow.

Obie cut wood for winter on Sunday. He bypassed dinner, saying he had more work, skipped supper to soak his blistered hands in the creek. And he chose to sleep in the barn instead of his bed, telling Chaser, "I'd sooner sleep with Stonewall the rest of my life and pick corn out of horse-droppings than I would set foot in her house."

The books that Mrs. Middleton sent home, Obie returned with Josh on Monday morning. A boy from hill country didn't need to know more numbers than what he could count on his fingers; didn't need to know how to spell *pneumonia* or *Mississippi;* didn't need to read newspapers or know about things going on in the world. Only thing the Immortals had saved him for was to be another dumb hillbilly. And Obie flung his only pair of shoes as far away as he could throw. Didn't need those either.

He spent the morning repairing the barn roof. He picked apples and ate them under the tree rather than going to the house for the noon meal. Didn't have anything to say to his mamma; didn't want to listen to any of her plans for the extra money.

Walls inside the root cellar and broken wires on the south pasture fence were mended when Josh and his sisters came up the road from school. Josh ran ahead to give Obie a note from Mrs. Middleton, but Obie tore it up without reading a single word.

"Whatcha do that for?"

" 'Cause I wanted to. Now, leave me be."

"You're acting just like Mamma," Josh yelled.

And Delsie added, "Getting to be just as nasty, too."

Obie stirred up a puff of dust as he swung around. He thought about their criticisms but dismissed them just as he had dismissed Mrs. Middleton's note. He saw no reason to go to church, no reason to return to school, no reason to try and better himself. He was all he would ever be . . . a dumb hillbilly. The Lord and the Immortals took care of that.

On Tuesday, Wednesday and Thursday Obie shucked corn. On Friday he shot the red hog with his daddy's old rifle. Used his granddaddy's skinning knife to slit its throat. With Orvull's help they doused the hog in boiling water to make the scraping easier. By evening the pig hung inside the springhouse, dressed and the carcass propped open to cool.

Mattie Mae fried pig's liver for supper. She talked about sewing a new quilt, about buying four heifer calves, about the kettle of apple butter cooking outside. She sang hymns as she rocked Loranda, took time to listen to Caleb recite his ABC's and hear Selena's prayers.

Obie hated her for being so happy, hated her for making him responsible, hated himself for not running off the way Virg had. And Obie chose to sleep in the barn another night.

When he awoke Saturday morning, he found his mamma's best blanket thrown over his shoulders. He flung it back, flung it into the far corner of the loft. "Damn you," he hissed. "Damn you!"

But he did the morning chores, filled the wood box and put Silas out to pasture. On his way back to the house, Obie saw a black roadster coming up the rutted road. He stopped, waited until he recognized Mrs. Middleton before glancing toward the house. He expected his mamma to step out on the porch, fire his daddy's old rifle in the air. Instead, he saw her slip back inside and peek from behind the corner window.

"Obie"—Mrs. Middleton waved—"you promised to show me the view from Addie's Ridge."

Obie recalled telling her that he always went to the ridge to do his thinking; he didn't remember telling her that there was anything up there to see except Wilks Hollow. But he waited and watched as she came closer, a paper tucked beneath her arm.

He studied the tilt of her head, the sunlight glistening on her reddish brown hair. She looked fresh-scrubbed and wore color on her lips. She smiled more than any woman he knew, laughed, too—laughed a soft, husky sound, like a mare nickering to its foal.

"I've missed you," she said. Then without giving Obie time to explain or time to unleash his frustrations, she said, "Josh told me how you were seeing to the needs of your family."

"Did Josh tell you that Virg stole my pearls and ran off to California?"

"Yes."

"I was going to use those extra pearls to pay my way north, help me get settled. I was going to make something of myself." Obie bit his lip to keep from crying.

"I know," she said, "Delsie told me that you were planning to work with your uncle at the automobile plant."

"Uncle Tully's real high-up; told me he could get me a job any time I wanted."

Her brown eyes settled over Obie. She slipped an arm around his. "Will you show me Addie's Ridge?"

Obie chose the long way to the ridge rather than the short, steep path. He took a deep breath, discarding the familiar morning smells, clinging to the scent of Mrs. Middleton's perfume. And he moved his arm so that he sometimes felt her hand press against his ribs.

Obie never thought of her as being a *nawthern woman* but he did think of her as being different from the other women in Graysonia. She looked fresh, young, alive. Why would such a woman ever come to a no-account place like Graysonia?

Once they reached the ridge, Mrs. Middleton turned in a circle before saying, "It's beautiful from up here."

Obie saw the same things—ridge lines that looked like a skinny man's spine; far off mountains that looked soft like velvet cloth; gray haze that made it all look fuzzy and unreal. "Don't look so beautiful to me."

"Perhaps you're not seeing everything or looking far enough ahead."

"It's the same no matter how far I look."

"You're wrong," she said. "One day you'll see it differently; you'll look at it with a giving heart."

Before Obie could respond, she stepped past him and moved farther up the hill. He hurried to catch up, wanting to argue rather than understand. He wanted to yell out all the injustices done to him, shout out his hatred for those responsible. He wanted to cry. Instead he pinched his lips tight and buried his disappointment deeper.

"Tell me about River Country. Tell me all about your adventure, every detail."

Obie began slowly and without enthusiasm. When he finished, he said, "I can't figure out why those Immortals spit me out of the sucking pot. Not a good thing has happened to me since I got back to this place." Obie wanted to curse. He wanted to yell "dammit"! He wanted to cry, run and hide.

"Obie, there can be more in your future than Michigan. There are many possibilities right here. You can be all that you want to be. More than you can possibly imagine."

Obie's lips pinched tighter.

"It's true," she said. "There are opportunities here, opportunities without the distractions that can take up and waste years of a young man's life. In a way, Obie, you're very fortunate."

"Fortunate?" All of the smoldering anger finally boiled over. "My own brother stole my share of the pearls; my own mamma and her younguns are stealing my life and this . . . this here hollow is taking away every chance I have to make something of myself."

"No. Nothing or no one can take your chances away from you. You're in control of your future."

But Obie chose not to hear and lashed out, "I went looking for those pearls to help out my family and to help myself, too. Except I ended up helping everyone but me. I hate this place," he yelled. "I hate everyone here. I'll never be any more than the same dumb hillbilly my daddy was."

"That's not true," she said. "You can make your life whatever you want it to be."

"What I want it to be? Look"—he flung out his arm—"there's nothing here. You've lived in Graysonia long enough to know that this is a nowhere place."

"There's no such thing as *a nowhere place.* But there are people who always choose to look at all that's wrong with a place and its people rather than focusing on all that's good."

Sun shone down on her hair and turned it a glistening red. "Obie," she asked, "just what do you want to do with your life?"

Obie studied the ridge lines, the far off mountains and the haze that made it look unreal. Mrs. Middleton's question hung inside the thickness. *Do with my life . . . ?*

"I want out of this place," he blurted. "I want to be someone special like my uncle Tully."

"Your uncle Tully? Tell me, Obie, just what did your uncle ever do for you or your family?"

Mrs. Middleton's question made Obie spin away, made him run up toward the ridge top. Finally he stopped. He looked in every direction before he settled down to focus on the pond below. He watched the fish swimming in circles, always confined by the limits of the pond. They had no other place to go. Like him, he thought. Then he looked up.

He saw her standing a few feet away. She held up a newspaper so he could read the headlines: AUTO-MOBILE PLANTS CLOSE: THOUSANDS JOBLESS: DEPRESSION SPREADS.

"Even if you had reached Michigan and your uncle, you wouldn't have found a job. You'd be standing in bread lines, sleeping in doorways. That's not what you want. That's not why you were saved from the sucking pot."

She sat beside him. "Whether you believe this or not, you already are someone special. Everyone is talking about what you and Bas did. You've given people hope." She paused, as if allowing him time to absorb her meaning. "My sister, who lives in Williamsburg, heard about your resourcefulness. Your story is in the Knoxville newspaper. Obie"—she placed a hand over his—"you still have the same opportunities to be somebody special as you had when you set out to find those pearls."

"You don't understand," he said, "I found those pearls because I had a map telling me where to go."

"I'll draw you a new map. A map guaranteed to make you that special person you want to be."

"How you gonna do that?"

"Simple. The map begins here in Wilks Hollow, graduation from high school, college—"

"College? Mrs. Middleton, that's pie-in-the-sky talk if I ever heard it."

"Why?" She waited, then continued. "You took a chance with that old map, didn't you? All a map does is take you from one place to someplace new—from Graysonia to Iversol, from high school to college."

Obie laughed. "There's no way a fellow like me will ever get himself to college. Mrs. Middleton, I'm a hillbilly. Hillbillies don't go to college."

"Why not? All it takes is the same effort and determination that it took to find those pearls. But you do have to want it."

"Wanting it is one thing. Paying for it is another," Obie said. "My mamma's got no money for sending me to college."

"There are scholarships, Obie. Scholarships that are given to the deserving regardless of where they come from."

Obie broke a twig from the hickory tree, snapped it in half. *Scholarship . . . college . . . ?*

He turned the two words over in his mind a second and third time. He repeated them silently until they began to take root, until they became more than just words, until they became possibilities. *College . . . scholarship . . .*

Me, Obadiah Wilks, a college graduate, me from up Wilks Hollow?

He measured the two pieces of hickory. Finally he drew a long, deep breath. "Reckon I've never thought on college, not for the likes of me anyways. But I kinda like the idea. Yes, ma'am, it sounds like a fine thing for me to be doing."

She stood. "I'll help you." She brushed at the wrinkles across the front of her skirt. "You would make an excellent teacher. You might like being an extension agent. One day you might even consider politics."

"Me? Politics?" Obie laughed. "Mrs. Middleton, I can't even talk Mamma into being civil to the Allardices. And Bas is fine folk."

"Sometimes, Obie, when reasoning fails you simply resort to telling."

Obie gave her a quick look. Mrs. Middleton was the smartest woman he knew but she didn't know the likes of Mattie Mae Wilks. His mamma had a stubborn streak wide as any six jackasses stood side by side.

"Will I see you in school Monday?"

Obie nodded. He followed her down the path to the car, opened the door, closed it when she slipped inside. "Would you say that if a fellow was thinking on a future, dealing with people, that it would be wisdom to learn the ways of reasoning and telling?"

She smiled. "See you on Monday."

Obie waited until her car disappeared before he glanced toward the house. He saw the curtain at the kitchen window swing back across the glass, knew his mamma had been watching, knew how spiteful she could be. Any woman stubborn as six jackasses was not going to like being ordered about.

Obie hitched up his overalls. Didn't know if teaching school or politics was what the Immortals saved him for but Obie wanted to be known for helping out rather than a fellow who never repaid his debts. "Yes, sir," he said as he started to the house, "besides being known as the best pearl finder in the state, I'll grow up useful, a fellow folks can count on to be a good friend."

CHAPTER

19

✳ ✳ ✳

OBIE TOOK THE PORCH STEPS IN ONE LONG LEAP. HE reached out for the door handle. He knew his mamma waited inside at the stove, stirring the pot of beans with the old, long-handled spoon. But instead of twisting on the knob and pulling open the door, Obie hesitated. All the courage that had sent him bouncing down the hill and filled him with the determination to *tell* his mamma instead of reasoning with her somehow got shook loose and lost.

He stepped back from the knob, feeling as empty as a hollow tree. He chewed on the inside of his cheek while words bounced around inside his brain. He tried stringing the words together so they would have some sense about them. But not a one of them was as powerful as his mamma's stubborn streak.

"When reasoning fails you resort to telling" was what Mrs. Middleton had said, but Obie had never done any *telling* to his mamma. Pussyfooting around her sour stares

and that way she had of looking right through him as if he had never been born was what he did best.

Obie sat on the top step. Chaser crawled out from under the house and sat beside him. Obie stretched his legs straight, the way he remembered his daddy doing. Crossed one foot over the other. Instead of sticking a corncob pipe between his teeth, Obie used a splinter of wood from one of the porch boards. He bit down hard. He looked off toward the creek like he remembered his daddy doing. But all Obie heard banging inside his brain was his mamma's silence and tapping foot.

Obie blew out his lips. Instead of telling her like he knew he should do and like he wanted to do, he thought of sneaking off the way his daddy always done, staying until past dark, past time his mamma could stay awake, then sneaking home and hiding the night in the barn.

"Dang bust it," Obie said and ran his hand the length of Chaser's spine. "Mamma's got a streak in her fierce as any Nun Yuna Wi." And telling her flat-out that he he was going to Felker Mountain to visit with Bas was more scary than the thought of wrestling a she-bear with cubs.

Obie studied the line of the split-rail fence. He followed the curvature of the barn roof as it cut across the morning sky. He even watched a hawk circle overhead, watched it soar with the air currents, then swoop down after a little mouse.

Obie felt like the mouse, thought of his mamma as the sharp-eyed hawk, quick and ornery, never letting anything grow up between her and what she wanted.

Obie planted a palm on each knee. He leaned forward, pushed up and stood. Then, like his daddy always done, Obie tucked a thumb behind the suspenders on his overalls.

"Mamma," he called, same as his daddy done, "I need to be talking with you."

Obie pushed open the door, wrinkled his forehead, the same as he remembered his daddy doing, and looked real thoughtful, just like the Good Lord Himself had been whispering in his ear. Then, nudging Chaser ahead, Obie followed his dog inside.

Mattie Mae raised her brow at the sight of Chaser slinking past the table leg, her belly so low that it was dusting the floor as she hightailed it for under the stove. Mattie Mae reached for the broom. "Mamma," Obie said louder than usual, "I got something real important that needs saying."

Mattie Mae let the broom handle fall back against the wall. She looked at Obie in a quizzical way, then at the floor and Chaser's tail, swishing back and forth. Obie watched her tail, too, and wondered what she had to be so dang pleased about. Soon as his mamma got to it, that warm spot under the stove would just be something Chaser could think about.

Obie felt Mattie Mae's eyes burn through his skull, pick at his brain just like a buzzard would do. And he said, "Mamma, I got something real important that needs saying."

"Seems to me, Obadiah, you just got done saying that very thing."

Obie chewed on the inside of his cheek. "Yes, ma'am, you're right as rain." Obie's head bobbed up and down. "I been thinking, Mamma, been thinking real hard on this here dislike you got bristling inside you for the

Allardices. It ain't good for you, Mamma. I read in the Bible that forgiveness is the way of the Lord. It says we got to love our neighbors."

"Obadiah Wilks"—she raised one hand to her hip, threatened him with the spoon from the pot of beans with the other—"don't you be preaching none to me, you hear."

"Mamma—"

"Your daddy's dead 'cause of them no-good moonshiners."

"Mamma—"

"I told you, Obadiah, they're not to set foot on my land. If that Bas is fool enough to try my patience—"

"I know," Obie said, his voice softening to a whisper, "you'll shoot him, maybe even kill him."

Obie pushed both hands into his pockets, raised his gaze from the floor where Chaser's tail lay still and silent to his mother's eyes. Their cold emptiness made him shiver. He knew that reasoning with her was a silly waste, and he said, "After you shoot Bas dead, what then, Mamma? You gonna order me to drag him off across the hollow, then lie when the law comes asking their questions? That what you want of me? That what it will take to make your heart peaceful?"

Mattie Mae's nostrils flared while the set of her thin lips made her look old, worn out.

Obie bit the inside of his cheek again and again, chewed on it until he tasted blood. Part of him was pushing to sneak away, give in to her meanness, wait his chance, then run off like Virg ran off. That part told him a scholarship and college were dream things, things from Mrs. Middleton's dreams, not his. But another part of him was mad. He felt the anger boil up, roll and churn around until a prickly itch made him step closer, meet his mamma's stare squarely. "The important thing I come to tell you is that I'll not be here for the noon meal. Me and Chaser are going up Felker Mountain to visit Bas and his daddy."

Mattie Mae's eyes thinned to dark slits; her face turned sour as spoilt milk. "You go up to that mountain, Obadiah Wilks, and I'll—"

"Mamma"—Obie raised his finger—"I'll not listen to any of your threats. If you want me here to help out, I'm willing, but you'll not be running me the way you done Daddy."

Muscles in Mattie Mae's chin quivered. Her lips drew tight against her teeth, and Obie said, "Mamma, I got no idea why you got so much meanness locked inside you, why you think us Wilkses is so much better than other folks. We ain't, Mamma. Ain't a one of us done nothing worth spit. Uncle Tully . . . he's the—"

Obie stopped short of saying *sorriest*. Morning was getting on. "One day real soon I'll be asking Bas to come down, maybe even ask him to stay to supper. I know you're gonna treat him good as kin, Mamma, 'cause if you don't—"

Again he stopped short. He felt a thin line of sweat trickle down his spine. Wasn't right of him to threaten her. Didn't want her to lose no sleep worrying over him running off. ". . . 'cause if you don't, Mamma, folks is gonna go on thinking us Wilkses is uppity and that won't be good. Soon as those heifer cows you're fixing to buy grow up, you'll need to do some trading, maybe even selling and buying. Mamma, you can be just as important

213

in these parts as Mr. Arvis Cagley. You can have folks liking you 'stead of having them think on you the way they do him."

Obie gave Mattie Mae a quick kiss on the cheek. "See you 'fore dark."

As Obie stepped to the door, he slapped his leg. He heard Chaser's nails click against the floor as she came out from under the stove, then heard his mamma say, "You keep that no-account pot-licker outta my house. Ain't gonna have her smelling things up, leaving her fleas to crawl on us."

Mattie Mae followed Obie to the door. "An' you best not be planning on the younguns doing your chores, you hear. You got responsibilities, Obadiah Wilks, and don't you be forgetting it."

She slammed the door. The air left Obie's lungs in a rush. For a moment he thought he might never catch his breath again. "Dang," he whispered before jumping to the ground, slapping his thigh for Chaser to follow.

She barked and ran ahead. Obie shook his head while disbelieving what he had just done . . . stood up to his mamma, stood up for himself like his daddy never done.

Obie crossed in front of the springhouse. He thought about his daddy, wondered why he never stood up to Mattie Mae, yet thinking he understood why. Dalton Wilks could outwork any five men living but he couldn't outtalk a-one. And Mattie Mae had a way with stringing words together, a way that tripped up and hog-tied a fellow until she had him believing he was lower than a snake's belly.

Obie followed the path toward Addie's Ridge. If all it took to quiet his mamma was a way with words, then

Obie felt blessed. And when he ran out of his own words, he knew Mrs. Middleton would teach him more.

Obie smiled. He called out to Chaser, then threw a stick for her to fetch. *A scholarship maybe . . . college . . . all the words he would say to his mamma and the new ones he would surely have to learn . . .* were those reasons enough for the Immortals to have saved him?

Were there others?

"Obadiah Wilks," he shouted, "I do believe your mind runs on just like Bas said it done, asking questions you got no answers for, questions that don't even make a lick of sense."

Obie laughed at himself, laughed until he recognized Sarson Allardice's cabin and saw the curl of smoke winding up from the chimney. "Bas," Obie called, "Bas Allardice, Chaser and me come a-visiting you."